Dark the Halls

TIMOTHY RODERICK

The story is a work of fiction. All all names, characters, incidents, organizations and dialogue portrayed in this novel are products of the author's imagination and are use fictitiously. No identification with actual persons (living or deceased), places, buildings, organizations and products is intended or should be inferred.

Published by Graven Image Press, Los Angeles, California

ISBNs

eBook: 979-8-9930845-0-3

Paperback: 979-8-9930845-1-0

First edition

Cover Design: © Graven Image Press

Printed in the United States

10 9 8 7 6 5 4 3 2 1

www.gravenimagepress.com

TIMOTHY RODERICK

ONE

"Marley was dead: to begin with. ... This must be distinctly understood, or nothing wonderful can come of the story I am going to relate."
                      --Charles Dickens, A Christmas Carol

A package arrived at his door. It was an odd-shaped parcel. Brown as autumn, flat, tied in red velvet ribbon and stabbed clean through with a sprig of holly. He might not have noticed it, lying on its side near the entryway, hidden by bushes.

It was a gray morning in Hollywood. Too gray, too low, too cold, even for sorrow. Someone rang the bell and vanished, leaving only the rain-dappled box.

It wasn't what he'd hoped. His heart stuck in his throat when the bell rang. It was always possible that more waited behind that door. Love returned to him. Some proof that all was not lost. But the stoop was dark, lit only by a reluctant sun fighting its way through the storm-worn sky.

If it weren't for the package, he'd have thought it was a child's prank on Christmas morning.

Rain had thundered through the Hollywood hills the night before. Rare in this place of dry riverbeds and parched, scrubby hillsides where green came only in the early spring. When the downpour came, he saw it as a sign. An omen. A Christmas miracle. But no.

Only the strange little gift.

Inside the wrappings, he found a note penned in an ornate script:

> *Dear Sir, If you will, bring the enclosed item to Cine-Film Finch and Malvern Studios, Screening Room Six. There, you will find everything you need, and all will be explained.*

It appeared to be signed by Mister Finch. *Mister Finch*.

That was impossible. Finch would've sent nothing more festive than an invoice or a subpoena.

The phone rang, and he felt his heart leap through his skull.

Since the crash, he and his mother could no longer afford the services of *Pacific Telephone and Telegraph*. The men came one day and removed the heavy black equipment and the cords that stretched deep in the walls. His mother knew this day would come, as it did for many. Bacon and eggs were priorities. Keeping a roof over one's head. Paying the electrical. Phone service was a luxury now.

Still, she kept secret the telephone hidden in the attic. A neighbor who was handy with tools and electrical devices took pity on the two of them and placed it there himself, without Pacific Telephone and Telegraph knowing. It was not customary to have more than one device in the home. To have two might have tipped the authorities of illegal book-making or other outlawed activities.

His grandmother lived and died in that attic in her infirmity. They were lucky enough to snag the upper floor of a house divided into four.

The dusty attic came with their portion, and since his grandmother's burial, neither he nor his mother felt a need to visit the stuffy room at the top of the narrow stairs.

The phone rang again.

He tucked the package under his arm and scrambled up the creaking, splintered steps.

He picked up the bell-shaped earpiece from the candlestick phone and listened.

There was breathing. Labored and wheezing.

"Nicky... Nicky is that you?" he asked.

The phone crackled and popped.

He whispered to the receiver. "Nicky? Can you forgive me? I was an idiot."

There was more breathing and electrical sputtering. The air was still, but the cold he felt started from beneath his skin.

He tried again. "Are you coming by today? It's Christmas."

From the other end of the line came static and a small, faraway voice.

"*Screening Room Six*," it said.

The line disconnected.

"Hello? Hello?" he asked.

He clicked the switch hook and called Nicky's name, but the line was dead. Then he saw the cord connecting the phone to the wall and noticed it was frayed all the way down. Mice loved the electrical cords for the braided fabric insulation. He followed the cord to its terminal end and saw they had chewed it through. Severed, and dangling from the tabletop onto a floor faded and powdered with a fine gray coating, connected to nothing but mouse droppings.

The young man sat in the studio alone. The walls sweated with age, and the air refused to move. He'd taken his mother's keys and passed the gate with a nod to the night guard at *CineFilm Finch and Malvern Studios*. No one would question him. He'd known them all since he was a boy. That made entering easy enough.

But there was no Screening Room Six. And he hadn't seen any new construction on the lot. But once he made his way to the editing suites, there it was, above the door. Proof of its existence.

Inside, the screening hall was vacant, silent as the wee hours, and the wall sconces flickered as though the power was throttled. Someone had already been there. They'd set the place up with a reel-to-reel projector. For him. They knew the contents of the strange Christmas package. Inside was a film wound around a cold black reel.

From inside the screening room, he phoned his mother. "I think you should see this."

He fitted it onto the projector, threading the film through the gears with care. His mother taught him how to do that when he was just a child. He recalled the days when Finch and Malvern sat shoulder to shoulder in this room, cigars puffing and trading snide remarks over every scene. And he'd sit on the floor, waiting to change the reel for them, with popcorn as his payment.

As soon as he hooked the film through the final sprockets, the projector whirred to life on its own, as if summoned by some ghostly intention.

"Hello?" he asked. But no one responded, except for Mister Finch, whose thin, lined face flickered upon the screen at the far end of the small viewing room.

The film was grainy and harsh, recorded in a black-and-white that bled at the edges. It was almost homemade—not what he'd come to expect from one of the leading studios of its day. Finch's image materialized from the screen's darkness. He was halting and in pieces at first. The sound was scratchy and full of static.

"This is how it began. The fall. My fall," Finch said. "You know this tale. It is nothing new. But how it came about and how it ended… these I kept in shadows. So, my gift to you is the truth in its entirety. There will be talk, but it is best if you know what happened beyond the side-whispered gossip."

The image of Finch stilled, gazing directly at the young man in the audience. He wondered if there was anyone else there, so he turned around. The theater remained empty.

"Hello. Are you listening?" Finch asked.

"You're… talking to me?" the young man asked.

His jaw locked into a silent gasp. It couldn't be. He didn't believe in ghosts. But, here in this deserted studio room, the air was heavy with an unseen presence. It wasn't just Finch's face, which was staring through the screen at him. That could have been a cinematic trick. But there was more. A weight in the room. A watching thing. Maybe more than one.

Finch continued.

"Mister Malvern was dead, and he had been for some time. Burnt to ash. And that was by design. I wanted him forgotten. I wanted him lost in the haze and blaze of old Hollywood searchlights, where the glare would be too bright for anyone who might come around snooping. Too dazzling for anyone to see what was really there.

"But a crematorium's fire can't erase truth. And neither can spectacle. Ash remembers. It clings to the air, to the walls, to the heart. And sweeping it away? Try your best. It will always refuse.

"In the end, even a searchlight will guide the curious of mind and will illuminate truth.

"Understand this and never forget it: Malvern was dead. Otherwise, my story will serve no end.

"It was October when things began to unravel. Perhaps it started much sooner. But for simplicity's sake, the wheels began turning on that fateful day in 1929: Black Monday. The markets collapsed. And so did men's nerves. Fear crept in colder than any autumn wind.

"That's when this tale took shape.

"That's when silence and shame, secrets and sorrow gave way to consequence. And the dead came calling. Oh, yes. Those who we think have gone to oblivion or to their final reward are never far... they're always there, just behind you now. Listening, watching, taking the final tally."

The young man leaned back, his eyes transfixed as the screen and its soundtrack crackled and split, opening to a different scene.

Those who had the misfortune of serving under either Mister Malvern or his rather questionable partner, Mister Finch, were near-unanimous in their view: Malvern was levelheaded, above all. He was a man not given to aimless wandering. And so, when he did wander—and thereby met his end because of it—it struck them not only as tragic, but utterly uncharacteristic.

The pair had produced a number of moving pictures since first witnessing a demonstration in Paris of the *Cinématographe*, a contraption that projected sixteen photographs each second, creating the uncanny illusion of life in motion. In time, and with a string of box office successes to their name, they fashioned a well-oiled empire, one that helped shutter more than a few vaudeville houses. CineFilm Finch and Malvern Studios.

It was not their fault; the march of time, the rush of progress, would have advanced with or without them. But they profited handsomely through scheming, through shrewdness, through knowing where to dig and where to bury the bodies of those they'd trampled. None more so than Mister Finch, whose ascent owed nothing to fancy, but everything to relentless defiance rooted in the hard soil of paternal disdain.

In the years before the crash, they had witnessed the slow demise of vaudeville. As crowds dwindled and laughter dimmed, they waited. Finch and Malvern loitered like crows upon a wire, ever watchful for the moment to descend.

They let the theater owners squirm, let them sweat through unpaid bills and withering receipts. They waited until the theaters were vacated entirely, their names struck from the city records, their doors nailed shut and listed for auction. Then they swooped, offering pennies on the dollar, and refitted the bones into glittering picture palaces.

And after the crash, those who lost their steady incomes from rat-a-tat-tat show business went broke. Jugglers and ventriloquists, tap dancers and pale-faced magicians fell to the margins. Breadlines took their bow. Pockets turned inside out.

Malvern was gone by then, and Finch was careful not to cast a backward glance that any might discern.

Those who attended Mister Malvern's graveside service whispered that he was once devoted to the written word and skilled with a pen. But under the steady influence of Mister Finch, whose ambition knew no rest, he became consumed with the studio itself and all its artifices.

He turned his attention wholly to the glare of the lights, to the whirl of the cameras, to the ceaseless machinery of spectacle. He allowed the ordinary affections and concerns of his life to recede into the wings, much like the straggling vaudevillians he and Finch allowed to fall into that purgatory of the theater where the show never starts, the house is empty, and the dressing rooms smell of mothballs instead of greasepaint.

On the dreadful day of Malvern's demise, Mister Finch recounted that Malvern rose from his desk after receiving a series of grim telephone calls which confirmed that his fortunes were, at last, extinguished. He shambled into the night, after first consuming whatever bottled consolation remained within his reach.

Finch told the authorities that Malvern walked as one entranced. His gaze was fixed heavenward, as if he beheld angels or Christ Himself, and he gave no heed to the thunder of trolleys nor the rush of approaching motorcars.

And as one might expect, it was not long before Malvern found himself under a streetcar, severed into butcher's portions and decapitated to boot. After the final wheel had done its job, only a gruel of gristle and a paste of flesh remained on that street.

The city took great care of the driver in question, lest he remain spooked by men darting across intersections. After scrubbing the blood from his shoes, wrapping him in a municipal blanket, and plying him with corned beef and cigarettes, they placed him in a quiet room with other drivers who'd had similar incidents so they could commiserate.

And there he stayed for the remainder of his days.

It was nearly Christmas, and it was a bitter one at that, by the time the coroner had pieced together enough of the grisly particulars to notify Mister Finch, who had been named to claim poor old Malvern's pulverized remains.

No family stepped forward to collect Mister Malvern's paltry assortment of giblets, and Mister Finch was by reputation and all appearances his brother. He was the obvious choice in the matter.

Naturally, Finch perpetuated the fiction of their fraternal relationship, a typical practice of the time. There was profit in it, a legal notary once assured the two of them. And he believed that after years of working together, it was not wrong to make such a statement. Others who knew the pair said they shared the same congenital malformation: a shrinkage of the heart.

Finch hadn't felt it as such, nor had he considered any shared coronary blackness. And in effect, it was accurate enough. Their film empire guided every thought, interaction, and word. They deemed all else unworthy. And while such a narrow view might seem suffocating, it resulted in bank accounts fattened beyond good taste.

Though he gave every appearance of composure, those who knew Mister Finch noted that his humors darkened after Malvern's loss. They hardened into a hunger for recognition and a thirst for legacy. And many said that he'd packed the cash the pair had amassed into the red-flocked walls of his home, certain no ruin would touch his secret hoard.

So, when the ravages of the market collapse fell upon others, when fortunes vanished and men leapt from ledges, Finch chuckled into his derby and ordered a second helping of shepherd's pie from *Cole's Dine-On-A-Dime*, just two blocks from where poor Malvern met his untimely demise.

Mister Finch saw to it that a coffin was lowered into the earth upon the occasion of his late partner's graveside service. That contrivance, grander than anything Malvern might have chosen for himself, contained only a jar of his favorite pâté and a few writing samples Finch considered fit only for lining a birdcage. Along with the vessel, Finch consigned his secrets to the earth that day, or so he hoped.

The mourners, faces drawn with the weariness of obligation, had no inkling. Finch, at the last, could not abide the thought of Mister Malvern's limited remains rotting and peeling beneath the earth. Ash was preferable; pliant, uncomplaining ash, which he could keep near, unnoticed, beneath the illusion of farewell. And so it was: the man who had once dreamed of building kingdoms upon celluloid was reduced at last to a handful of soot, confined within a funereal urn, unable to protest long business hours or to collect another paycheck.

Still, the cold had a way of creeping in, not through the seams of flocked wallpaper or the lining of a casket, but through the stitches of the soul. And Finch, bundled in his woolen coat and spotless bowler, felt it keenly as he made his way toward Saint Cyprian's Hospital to claim the remains of the man who had stood beside him longer than anyone else.

The hospital foyer smelled of boiled linens and antiseptic sorrow.

"What business have you here?" the nun asked.

She watched Finch with crepe eyelids and doubt. Finch thought she looked like someone who had once longed for something worldly, only to bury the want beneath starched vestments and a lifetime of carping. Finch knew he could neither charm nor cajole her out of her religious afflictions. He'd have better luck with a gargoyle atop Notre-Dame.

"I am here at the behest of Officer Laraby," Finch said.

He pulled the seal-skin collar up a bit after he felt a draft pull through the halls of the old hospital, and he produced the official paperwork, stamped with an embossed insignia of the Los Angeles Police.

"Sign here," the nun said.

She spun a wooden palette atop a dais near the old gate. Finch signed his name but noticed that his hand and the quill in it shook. He steadied it with his other black-gloved hand then stepped away from the podium. He wouldn't want anyone to see. He wouldn't want anyone to have a hint, even in the slightest.

She gazed at the signature with a slow eye and mouthed his name with a thick orange tongue that made her look as though she were a few short days from the grave herself.

"Bram-well? Bramwell Finch? They might as well have named you Dracula."

Finch spoke. "My father..." He cleared his throat. He felt his heart skip. He needed to maintain his composure. "Finch is a fine family name."

"But Bramwell. Who would name their child *that*?"

Finch recalled at that moment. He had never been to his father's liking. Not even to the end. His mother told him as a boy that his father first named him *Hideous*, but that did not last. The man likely chose his son's name to match his own bitter disappointment and soured disposition.

Finch stiffened and tapped his fingers on the podium.

"And yours? May I venture a guess? Sister Distemper? Sister Castor Oil?"

The nun stepped to the gate, her shoes squeaking as they scuffed against the checkered linoleum. The gate, which he supposed separated the vaulted, echoing lobby from the remainder of the hospital. She unlocked it with a loud clink, and she shuffled back to her station with an unsteady gait, hunched forward all the way as though studying the shoe scuffs she'd made just before.

"Nuns do not have personal names, Mister Finch. We shed such vanities at the door. The world has enough men chasing notoriety and personal attention. Weak. All of them. I dare say you know something about this. Weakness comes in many forms, Mister Finch. Pride, indulgence, appetite. But you, sir, have a particular reputation that precedes you. And it does not wear a halo."

"Oh? And how so?" he asked.

"There was a matter of donation, just this past year, Mister Finch," she said.

"Oh, but of course. No need to thank me. Please step aside," he replied.

"*Thank* you? Mister Finch, I do not find such flippant humor amusing. You never responded to our inquiries for help in purchasing additional iron lungs. They could have saved countless children. Many suffering the scourge of consumption or of infantile paralysis were left to gasp and clutch to their loved ones through their final days. Due to shortages, most could not afford the needed care, and once winter set in, once Christmas came around....? It was a dark season. And this year all the darker."

"Yes, Sister, and I've been rationing my pity by the thimble. I trust you'll understand. Now if I may attend to my business," Finch said.

Her eyes widened.

"Families have next to nothing since the crash, Mister Finch. The Sisters of Saint Cyprian rely on the charity of those more fortunate to meet even the simplest needs. The children have gone without all season. We have rooms without heat. Blankets as measly as bed sheets. One nurse for twelve dying tots...."

"Well, Sister, I can't very well be held personally responsible for any banking collapse, can I? Or for your church's poor accounting, or some rash investment? If I'm to be blamed, why not fault me for the tides or the earth's rotation? Darwin called it natural selection, did he not? Illness, poverty, these are nature's tools. We cannot mourn every soul that is pruned away, or we'd be weeping from cradle to coffin. No. Leave such matters in God's hands. Pray at the foot of the crucified Christ, dear Sister, and you'll be doing your work as well as any stockbroker. Now, may I pass to attend to my business?"

Her chin quivered, and he thought it a performance worthy of the silent pictures.

"Every deed carries its own merit or its debt. Whether you know it or not, Mister Finch, the account is still due," she said. Then she lifted her chin.

"Then I hope the good Lord takes cash," Finch replied.

"Take your business, Mister Finch, and be quick about it. We have no need for those who meet their toll with mockery, or the call for mercy with silence."

It was then that she locked her gaze upon him, that he noticed the white glaze of cataracts across her eyes. She swung the gate wide, and it screamed in pain on its metal hinges.

"We have rules here at Saint Cyprian's, Mister Finch," she said.

"Rules? You surprise me, Sister. I had you pegged for more of a jazz club girl," he replied.

She blinked but would not react more.

"We do not allow the smoking of cigarettes, pipes, or cigars. Is that clear?" she asked.

"Of course," Finch replied.

She glanced at the cigar stowed in his velvet vest pocket.

"This shall remain in my custody, unlit, much like your bedside manner," Finch replied. He patted his pocket and then removed his second glove.

"You do that," she said. "Do you know how many have died from lung ailments induced by the smoking of tobacco?"

"I imagine fewer than those who've died of boredom at your reception desk. You seem especially concerned about lung ailments, Sister. Perhaps you should take a few deep breaths. Though I imagine the air is thinner at your moral altitude. In any event, is it always your custom to detain visitors with endless questions when they are en route to claim the deceased, or am I a particular case?"

Her jaw clenched, but she kept a steady gaze on him.

"Likewise, we do not speak in the hallways," she said. "Those who are badly off must come here. We have no need for the likes of cane-walking dandies who make a commotion to wake the dead."

Her creased face seemed to sallow more than before Finch's arrival. Pucker marks deepened by the second around her lips.

"I shall remain silent as the grave."

Finch gave a wan smile.

"Coroners are down the hall. Turn left at the end. Then right. Then two lefts. Then another left and a right. Go through the first double door on the right. People have gotten lost here, and we don't have time to fetch them back. We have enough to do. Is that clear, Mister Finch? Have I made myself understood to you?"

"Exhaustively." He let the syllables drag on the floor.

"Fine, you may pass. I won't recite the directions again. I'm far too busy, Mister Finch."

She lowered her head and studied his name on the register once more, tapping a pencil on its yellowing pages.

"Pray for me, won't you?" he replied.

He strolled through the gates, and she closed them behind him with more hinge screams and a final clanging that sounded as though hell itself locked him in.

Outstretched was a long corridor, white walls, and a checkerboard floor. Doors lined the passage, each with a small rectangular inset window made of glass and wire mesh. He started ahead, marking his steps with his silver-tipped cane, and came to the first intersection and there he turned left. However, there was no right turn ahead, as Sister Lollipops described. He turned and backtracked. Instead of a left, he turned right around the corner. But ahead of him was an unfamiliar passage of checkered flooring stretching out the length of at least a long city block.

This couldn't be right. The building was compact from the street. It was efficient and logical, a point to which any architect would attest. It was just as he preferred his world to be. He hadn't taken a wrong turn, and he wouldn't believe it, even if Sister Sardines insisted he had. Buildings didn't shift, and neither did his mind. She had given false information, and that was long and short of it.

He would speak with her again, but the gate was nowhere in sight. It made no sense that he had walked only a short while and ended up so far. He felt a twinge; an unsettled flutter made itself known in his chest. Peculiar.

Given the journey back would take more time than he had allotted for this task, he continued to the left, in search of the promised double doors. After all, there were meetings to attend and production schedules to follow. He would have to complete the task of claiming Malvern's remains today, given that there was a cancellation in his planner, and Malvern's funeral would otherwise become that much more delayed. And the dead must have their rest, along with their stories.

The halls were silent, save for his echoing shoes and the tick-tick-tick of his cane. He also heard the occasional wail or weeping from behind those hallway doors. Curiosity got the better of him, and he approached one. Before peering through it, he glanced back along the corridor he'd come from.

From the count of his steps and the fatigue settling into his stride, he guessed he'd walked another half mile, maybe more. But that was impossible. He recalled the scene from the street. The entire building spanned a quarter of a block at most. This wasn't one of Horace Bellamy's feature reels, the kind that promised no escape, not even for the popcorn.

His heart hitched, and he felt a cold tingling like an electrical current coursing from the center to the periphery.

"Sister Humpty Dumpty?" he asked. "Hello? Anybody?"

His voice reverberated through the empty space, shaped by panic that coiled like a tightening snake around each word.

He peered into the window and saw Sister Distemper's pale, habited head protruding from an iron lung. He first tapped on the window with his knuckles, then his cane, following an involuntary gasp. The doorknob only jiggled, but the door remained shut.

"Sister. Sister, can you hear me? Where are the double doors?" He didn't know why he asked. She had just been speaking to him, and back at the gate she was whole and upright. Now this? He backed away, the cane loosening in his grip.

She remained with eyes shut. She was more a fixture than a person, unmoved by voice or gesture. He tapped the glass again with the metal cane end. Then again. He smacked the glass hard enough that it fractured.

A face surfaced in the glass, white and smooth as a snake's underside. The eyes staring back at him were dark, unblinking slits. He slipped in his spatted shoes and fell backward to the floor. His cane skidded away, and he scrambled to collect it, only then realizing he had lost his sense of direction.

Whatever he'd seen, it was unnatural, and he knew he was lost in those long, labyrinthine halls with that thing waiting behind the walls.

His mind raced to recall the path. First a left, then a right. Wasn't that it?

Doors faced one another along the hallway in perfect formation.

No matter, he thought. He could find his way with reason and a cool head. He'd find the very door he faced by the cracked glass, then he'd know from which direction he'd traveled. Malvern's body would have to wait another day or longer. Finch had spent enough time and trouble on the matter, and his stomach tightened from lack of a cheese sandwich, which he'd been craving since mid-morning.

He approached the door across from him, assuming it must be the likely candidate. He expected to find the fissure but discovered a window whole and untouched. Not even a fingerprint. He hurried to the window across the hall. And this, too, was unmarred. An uneasy prickle started under his skin. He'd continue in a direction. For now, any would do. Someone would find him, given enough time. He stepped up his pace, peering at every window along the hall. They all were undamaged.

He gazed through several of them, only to find empty gray rooms. No patients in bandages or casts. No cold compresses on foreheads. The rooms were also empty of beds and the usual hospital equipment. Instead, every cell had four bare walls, equipped with a single flickering bulb hanging from an exposed wire.

This facility offers more ruin than recovery, Finch thought.

He wondered if a donation might have been in order after all.

He realized he had stopped breathing. With that awareness came a series of sharp, ragged gulps, as if swallowing gallons of water. He quickened his pace, pretending he knew the way. But his confidence was as lost as he. His shoes creaked against the tile, the only echoes in a place empty of all life but his own.

Strange. He'd never heard his shoes make any sound before. For top dollar, he'd commissioned an Indian man to employ his child to hand-stitch them, creating tiny, perfect seams. Finch would have a word with him the next time an opportunity arose. Children ruined everything.

He'd walked the hallways for some time before realizing there were no windows. He'd keep going, though. Given time, he'd arrive at someone's desk or a stray iron lung. It was a hospital, after all.

Much further down, he caught sight of a nun. She was pale, ghostly, and dressed in white from head to toe. She floated across the hall as though gliding on ice and disappeared from view.

"Oh, Sister," Finch said. "Sister, one moment please."

He strode with lengthy, fought steps, each squeaking along, each louder than the last. He raised his cane, hoping to hail her down like a taxi on Sunset Boulevard.

The hallway lights blinked out, leaving him in absolute darkness. For a brief, breathless moment, he feared his body wouldn't move. His limbs might lock or fail him, and he'd be left standing there, alone, in the black. But he heard his shoes slapping and squeaking against the linoleum and his breath laboring as he ran.

Before him, a flood of light burst upon him. White, sterile, searing light. Finch held his hands up and shielded his eyes.

"Mister Finch," he heard.

He turned to the voice behind him. A doctor stood in a surgical gown and mask that strapped across his face and covered his nose and mouth. Wet black gloves coated his hands, shining as if rinsed in someone else's blood.

Finch gasped at the sudden light and held his cane up in a protective reaction.

"Mister Finch, please, sir. There's no need for that. Are you forgetting where you are?" the doctor asked.

Finch lowered his cane. As a man who knew the camera's angles and what differing perspectives might yield, he realized how he must have appeared. A man who'd lost his senses might stand so. His eyes refocused and he gazed around, noticing the cool green tile covering the surrounding walls. On the floor were rows and rows of wheeled gurneys, each with a sheet covering and clinging to the shapes of the bodies beneath.

"I thought... never mind what I thought," Finch said. A heat rose in him, not against the doctor, but at the fool he must have looked. It wasn't this man's fault. Still, someone had to bear the brunt of his bluster for the indignities of the hallway. "I am here to..."

"Yes, yes, yes. Of course, Mister Finch. We know why you're here," the doctor said.

He raised his hand, and in floated the nun Finch had previously seen. It was as though the vapors from stray ether lifted her an inch or two above the tiles. But he could not see what silenced her steps, as her robes covered her entirely and mopped the floor behind her.

"Sister Zagan, will you please wheel Mister Malvern to us?"

She nodded but did not speak. Her eyes remained lowered, which Finch presumed was a gesture of reverence or perhaps a way to conceal some secret. But when she flicked them upward, only for a moment, Finch saw them. They were set too far apart, the pupils slitted and empty, like those of a forest creature that watched with no trace of feeling. He had seen her. Yes, in the vacant room's window.

He staggered back and clapped a hand over his mouth.

"There, there," the doctor replied. "You must steady yourself, Mister Finch. A corpse cannot hurt you. Especially one as... fragmented... as Mister Malvern's. Though I must warn you, Mister Finch... we could salvage only a modest assortment: some gristle, shredded skin, a few loose bones, and, ah yes, Mister Malvern's head. The rest, well, I'm sorry to report, but the gulls pecked the remains away, and what they had not eaten, the city street sweepers brushed into sewers.

"Tragic, tragic, yes, tragic. And to bring you into these facilities to bear witness at this festive season... why, it must be quite disturbing for you. Quite disturbing. Still, we did not want to presume to sign the death warrant until we had a positive identity of what bits remain."

"Are there that many loose heads in Los Angeles that they are in danger of being mixed up?"

"You'd be surprised. We've got a whole drawer labeled *Possibly Eugene.*"

"In any event, I do not partake in the season, or in making merry," Finch said. He lifted his chin and gazed down his crooked nose at the doctor. He could not tell the man's reaction behind that green surgical mask, though faces he'd encounter often shifted to disgust or surprise. "Claiming Mister Malvern's remains is only an inconvenience insomuch as it takes time from my studio."

But even as he said it, he could feel his chest tighten and his lips flatten into a line. It wasn't grief. But there was an incessant crackle behind the ribs, like a broadcast he could not tune out. *They mustn't know. I must remain as stone*, he thought. There were vultures circling everywhere, waiting to call the tabloids, and he would not give any of them a morsel over which they could slaver.

"I quite understand, Mister Finch. Time, money. These are most important, most important indeed. After all, there are meetings to attend and production schedules to follow," said the doctor.

Finch shrank within himself. Those were his very thoughts just before he came upon the coroner's office. How could the man have known?

"And might I say, Mister Finch, I was rather partial to your picture, *Midnight Maracas* with Miss Lola Fontaine. Tell me, is she quite as... ahem... *robust* in person?" the doctor asked. He winked.

Finch lost all speech, but only long enough to collect his indignation. "Please, sir. May we proceed with the business at hand?"

"Yes, yes, of course. It's just that Miss Fontaine is such a favorite. She was especially good in *Congo Conga*. She certainly puts the motion in pictures, wouldn't you say?"

"Please, doctor!"

"Yes, of course, Mister Finch," the doctor said. He continued to lock his gaze with Finch's, which made Finch flinch. "No need to dilly-dally. Time, money, production schedules...." Each word landed like an anchor. Each one felt like a finger of blame. But how? Finch refused to look away. He cleared his throat instead.

The nun wheeled in a small metal table, not much more than the size of an examination tray. Beneath the white sheet protruded a bumpy mass. She whipped the sheet away with the flair of a bullfighter yanking away his cape, then she floated out the door with it tucked under her arm like a folded ghost.

Atop the metal tray sat Malvern's head. His eyes remained open and his mouth agape. His glazed, pale eyes stared ahead; a dried trickle of blood clung to a corner of his pouting, blackened lower lip. His neckline was a mess of pulverized bone fragments, with flesh still clinging to them like tissue once wetted, now dried.

Finch averted his gaze, unwilling to meet Malvern's eyes. For the first time, he felt a blow he couldn't deflect. It was a gut-wrenching grief that offered no weight, no measure, no profit. His breath, his words, his mind caught like a match failing to strike. His heart constricted, not with grief, but with a numbness so complete, anyone else might mistake it for frostbite.

Still, his eyes stayed dry. Crying, he reasoned, was for starlets with poor reviews and extras who never made the poster. Leaking eyes would not salvage the mess in front of him. It was done, and no one could undo it. There he was, staring back at Finch with cold, gelatinous eyes.

"Is it he?"

Finch nodded and turned his body away.

"Fine, fine. I would like you to complete this paperwork for the county records. You said you were his brother, did you not?"

Finch took a slow inbreath and felt a chill seep through his chest, through his limbs, like dampness infecting an old house. It sank into the grain of his cane, into the stitching of his gloves, into every thread of his coat until he felt engulfed by it. Yes, he was upright, breathing by all accounts, and no one would know with certainty his disquiet.

"Yes."

"And how is it you have such different surnames?"

"Because '*Finch and Finch*' would've belonged over a hardware store, not a film empire."

"Dear me. Such a story. Wait till I tell the Misses. Sign here. And here. And here. And here. I'll have Sister prepare a canister for poor Mister Malvern. We can send that to the mortuary of your choice."

Finch looked at the ground. It was finished. There was nothing of himself left to recognize after the doctor's words, only the silence that follows a final breath.

"Send these few pieces to the crematorium," Finch said. He could not make eye contact.

"And to what cemetery shall they send the ashes?"

"Cemetery? Amusing. Since Mister Malvern would have chosen production over pall bearers, marquees, over mausoleums, it is best if you have the ashes sent to my production offices, thank you."

He signed the doctor's papers and handed them over. The gowned physician promptly left Finch with Malvern's head while he toddled away with the signed paperwork.

Finch worked up his nerve enough to meet Malvern's unseeing gaze.

"So, this is how it ends, is it? Shreds and splinters. Dramatic to the end, I see," Finch said. He looked away, for it seemed the glazed eyes had an uncanny stillness to them that he could not tolerate. "Cemetery. Outrageous. You would not approve, Edmond. No, you would not."

From the far end of the sterile quarters came a rustling sound. A sheet. Yes, it was fabric moving. But he was alone in that room, surrounded by corpses.

Finch looked around and saw it. Near the door was a body, once lifeless, sitting with its spine taut and head tilted, like a puppet yanked upright and positioned by invisible hands. Finch removed a pair of spectacles he kept in his breast pocket and held them to his eyes. His heart fluttered, and his mind flew a million miles away. It was not possible.

Another body did the same, sitting upright, pulling against its sheet. Then another. And all of them in the room sat upright. Five in all with their coverings across their pale, cadaverous faces.

He stumbled backward into Malvern's tray-table. The head toppled to the floor and rolled around at Finch's feet until it came to rest, at length, with its eyes staring upward.

The head whispered, breathy but clear: "Fiiinch."

Finch shrieked and scrambled backward until he fell, clutching at what he thought was Sister Zagan's white robes. But where he thought to find white vestments, he found instead a white goat with four curling horns rising from its skull. Its hooves planted firm, it stretched high above him. Old blood crusted its pelt and dried around the mouth, matted into the beard and stiff across the chest. But fresh stains glistened, too, deep and red along the lips. They were the raw, livid shade of organ meat.

Finch howled and crumbled to the floor with his hands over his eyes.

"Mister Finch!" the doctor said. "Please get a hold of yourself... but where I would not know."

Finch gazed upward, and the goat he imagined towering above him was no more than Sister Zagan. He sniffled and stiffened his innards then pulled himself upright, placing a hand to his mouth. The bodies in the morgue remained as before, undisturbed, lying flat beneath their white coverings.

Mister Malvern's head still rested atop the tray, his eyes fixed in a vacant stare, as if trying to remember what it meant to be alive.

"But you don't understand. I stumbled and I saw... Didn't you see...?"

"We understand, Mister Finch. Claiming a deceased loved one in such a condition... why, it is bound to play on the nerves. Now, please follow Sister Zagan. We will send along Mister Malvern's effects to your studio, and Sister will see you safely to the gates. And Mister Finch...? See you in the pictures."

TWO

FIVE CHRISTMASES PASSED. TREES were cut and trimmed, withered, and crumbled to pine dust. The world moved on as it always did. Death came and went, with no one paying particular attention. Hospital beds rolled away. Paperwork was filed. And Bramwell Finch, having burned to ash what little remained of the past, returned to the business of tomorrow. His office was waiting. There were films to produce, budgets to manage. *Laurels* to collect and protect. And it seemed not every ghoul came from the coroner's office.

Lola showed up after hours, two nights before Christmas.

She slipped into the leather chair at the desk that was once Malvern's, situated across from Finch's own, and she toyed with the fur collar of her leopard-print dress. She looked like a jungle cat, if jungle cats wore rouge and worked the midnight shift on Sunset and Vine.

She eyed the vase near the middle of the desk. It was a vase in the same way Lola was a singer: too ornate and easily shattered. It was a black-and-white porcelain urn with frantic little vines of gold climbing their way up, and too many rogue florals planned to choke the thing. Two gilded nudes clung to either side, begging for attention, while the base was a garish square of gold and looked like someone had tried to reproduce Versailles on Malvern's desk.

He could see a crease starting in the middle of her brow.

"Creepy. Is that thing where you keep him now?" Lola asked. She shook her foot, and her glance was less easy than when she arrived.

"Perhaps we should stick to the matter at hand," Finch replied.

"I don't mean no disrespect, but couldn't you have moved him to a mausoleum?" she asked.

"I see no more fitting a tribute than to keep Mister Malvern at his desk where he wrote the very lines you sang in that withering rasp of yours," Finch said.

"Why, thank you very much," she said. She fluffed up the collar more. "I mean, I've never been to this office, except for when I signed my contract and... well, that other time, which was a mistake. It was a pure mistake, mind you." She eyed the urn and looked like she'd eaten a rotten cheeseburger. "Gosh, this is the first time I've even thought of him... in his current situation. You know what I mean? Current situation? I wouldn't have ever known or suspected what you'd done with the body, you know? Didn't you have him buried?" she said.

"Miss Fontaine. You're trying my patience," Finch said. He glowered at her.

"Okay, well, in that case, Finchy, let's talk business, shall we? And just so you don't waste your breath, if you're thinkin of offering the role of Queen Marie Aunt-Annette in *Lady Guillotine*, you'll have to understand that I come at a premium now. I mean, what's a girl to do with one picture like *Lady Guillotine*? Get a few mug shots in the trades? A little extra pocket change? Collect a Laurel? Times are tough, Finchy, and a girl needs to look after herself. So, I got to thinkin. I says to myself, 'Lola, you're a pretty shrewd businesswoman. Maybe you should be sittin across from Finchy.'"

"What?" Finch asked. The storm in his eyes darkened. Lightning was about to strike.

She stroked the fur of her collar as though she was soothing a pet.

"I mean, after all. I think I know enough after five pictures to run this place just as good as anyone. Much better than a dead guy in a vase, I'll tell you that," she said.

Finch rose, towering. He lit a cigar and let the smoke build between them. He offered her nothing but the dead, smokey air between them getting colder by the second and a satisfied grin like he'd eaten the last doughnut from a boxed dozen.

"You remember when we first signed you some years back?" he asked.

"Of course I do. What of it? As far as I can tell, Finchy, from today onward, we have a whole new arrangement," she replied. "I mean, what would the papers think if they *knew* what went on behind the scenes here? The audiences? It would just be devastatin. Why, I imagine with all the radio moralizing I hear, you'd be in a pretty tough spot."

Finch cleared his throat, chomped down on his cigar, and opened a manilla envelope that lay on the desk in front of him. From it he poured out playbills and photos of Lola. Most of them depicted her barely hiding her plump whatnots behind a white feather fan. A few black-and-white glossies that slid out were a bit more revealing.

"What do we have here, Miss Fontaine? I believe our *arrangement* was for five pictures, not a scrapbook full of tawdry peep shows," Finch said.

Lola sat up and grasped at the images and playbills. She gasped. Nearly choked. "It can't be... Where did you get these?"

"Quite the cash haul, wouldn't you say, Lola?" Finch asked. "Or do you still prefer *Boom-Boom Baxter*?"

"What?" she asked. She paled, like her face on a poster left to bleach and peel at some forgotten bus stop. "No..."

"Oh, yes," Finch said. "Burlesque at sixteen? Naughty, naughty, *Boom-Boom*. And some of these cheesecake photos.... For the sake of propriety, I'm only displaying the *nice* ones. I'm keeping the others for insurance purposes."

She stuffed as much as she could into her handbag, which yawned open and looked resentful of the abuse.

"Don't you try this with me, Finch. I remember *what I saw*. I remember the two of you here... alone in this office. That wasn't a mistake. I *know* what I saw. And if the public knew...."

"You saw nothing, you ungrateful toad. You saw what you *wanted* and thought a little pressure might get you somewhere. Well, let me tell you something, Miss *Baxter*... this is the end of the line at CineFilm. Even Scarlett Diamond is more relevant than you... and that's saying very little. So go cry to the press with your little blackmail fantasy. They'll laugh. The police won't. And after you're sued into oblivion and jailed for your activities, I'll still have boxes of programs, news clippings, and those luscious little French postcards that'll finish whatever's left of your career. Here! Take a few more, you scheming trollop."

He withdrew a box from under his desk, overflowing with memorabilia, and upended it—pages and photos spilled out like a paper waterfall, fluttering to the floor in a manic flapping.

The urn tipped, and its lid popped open. Ashes spewed across the desk and laid a thick powder across Lola's face. She coughed and dropped to her knees, panicked, tear-streaked, snapping up whatever she could and shoving it down the top of her dress.

She screamed. "Oh, my God!" She'd hit perhaps some of the finest notes in her career. She coughed and sputtered on the floor. "No... where did you get...? No!"

She sobbed, clutching at the mess with her thick red fingernails. Finch eyed her theatrics and felt nothing. Lola Fontaine had built her career on mascara, ambition, and more hot air than a radio soap opera, he thought. He never understood what Malvern saw in her.

He righted the urn and scooped up as much ash as he could with a nude photo of her holding a rope strategically in front of her this-and-that, and he shoveled it back into the urn.

"Go on! Take your souvenirs. Frame them if you like. Maybe they'll still fetch a nickel at a pawnshop on Franklin. I'll tell you this: they'll be the only thing you have left of your career after I'm through with you. Now get out!"

She wobbled to the door, gasping, scattering cremains across the floor, and gathering the last scraps of her dignity like spilled pearls. At the threshold, she paused, her shoulders trembling. She opened her handbag and reached deep, past the crumpled playbills and folded photographs. As she withdrew something wrapped in silk, a few of the photos fluttered to the floor. She held the object in her gloved hands as if it were a bird too fragile to wake. Then, she set it on his desk.

At first glance it looked somewhat like a crystal ball on a stand.

"I had a feeling you'd pull something dirty. Lucky for me, my grandmother taught me how to deal with men like you," she said.

Finch started, but before he spoke, she turned it over and wound the key.

The little toy tinkled a haunting, slow *Silent Night* and made an ominous turn.

Finch looked like he'd swallowed poison.

"Where? How did you...*find* that?" he asked.

"A little music to keep you company. You might find the tune... unforgettable. Merry Christmas, Finch."

She reeled down the steps, dropping photos and playbills like a drunk juggler exiting a vaudeville stage.

The music box stopped when the office door slammed shut behind Lola.

Finch eyed it for a moment then scraped it up from the table. He gave the snow globe a swirl, and the tiny white flakes fluttered around Father Christmas stationed at the center. Finch flipped it over and saw the golden oval insignia: *Marchette of Paris.* He hadn't seen that name in almost a lifetime. It had to be a coincidence.

"Poppycock," he said.

Without wasting another moment on Lola and her theatrics, he turned his attention to the mirror behind him. He straightened his tie. That finished that. One melodramatic cow down, and somehow, the evening was still young.

"Don't listen to any of them now, Finch," he said out loud. "All of them want to see you fail. With Edmond gone, they think you're next on the funeral pyre. Well, they've got another thing coming. I'm just hitting my stride."

He glanced down at Malvern's desk and saw a case of his favorite cigars, dusted with Malvern's own ash. Despite the mess, the office looked untouched, as though Edmond Malvern had simply stepped out and might return at any moment.

"Goddammit, Edmond. Just... goddammit."

Finch turned to the mirror and attempted a smile, but the gesture collapsed midway. His voice had sounded strange to his own ears. It carried a tremor, quiet but unmistakable. It was an echo of a door long shut beginning to unhinge.

It wasn't grief. Of course it wasn't. Just a bit of misplaced nostalgia, he thought, sneaking in with the cold. He had no time for such things. Nostalgia stayed longer than it ever should, and it made a fool of a man.

And after such thoughts came, a feeling dropped inside him, quick, sharp, now gone. The silence filling the room felt stifling. It was a silence that was always there, haunting in the background.

He glanced at Edmond's desk from the mirror, thinking he might find the man still sitting across from him, toasting with his one last Scotch belt before hitting the road. Straightening his bowtie and complaining that it was on too tight. Lola was Edmond's pick, so it was better he wasn't around to witness her inevitable spiral, or the lengths Finch had gone to cut the cord. But if Edmond knew of her accusation, he'd have likely done the same. Yes, Finch decided. Edmond would have done the same.

Finch hardened his stare at his reflection, and he thought about how much he looked like his father now. How much he'd aged since that night of Edmond's tragedy. He had to do it all by himself now. In a blink, the wound was opening. He'd have to pull off some quick emergency surgery if he was going to shine as they all expected in the coming hours.

"So what if he's gone now?" he said. He thought he sounded convincing. "It's you who matters now, isn't it? It's you that's always carried the headline. Writers, directors, actors all come and go. But you're still the king of this rotten little town. Now straighten up, pull yourself together, and go get that award."

Finch sat with his hands knotted together. He hid them under the white tablecloth so that washed-up drunk Vivian Delacroix wouldn't see how tightly he'd clenched them. Her performance in *A Kiss Before Dying* had earned her a nomination for best actress this year, and she had a fair shot at winning. She really hammed it up this time. She gave the critics plenty of eye rolls and faints to the floor that only an imbecile would find compelling. But her tight grip on the *Motion Picture Guild* assured her nomination, if not the award itself.

She looked him up and down from behind her golden lorgnettes. It wasn't so obvious that anyone but him might have noticed. But she stared just the same then lowered her glasses so that she might sip from an oversized martini.

"How are you doing, darling, Finch? It's been five years since... well, you know what happened. CineFilm just hasn't been quite the same since your dear Edmond took his final bow. It's like you've been a bit... lost."

She made a dramatic gesture while flitting a blue scarf. Her theatrics weren't for him, but for everyone else at the banquet who may have watched. She continued. "Lost in an ocean with no guiding beacon, one might say. Oh, such a pity. Though I suppose he's off in some celestial chorus now... assuming they take his kind," Vivian said.

"His kind?" Finch asked.

"Producers, naturally, darling. I thought they had a one-way ticket *elsewhere*," Vivian said.

She was having a hard time enunciating. How many martinis had she gargled since the gala began? Finch lost count when he ran out of fingers.

"Speaking of the sea, Vivian, you might want to pace yourself. Drowning in gin is such an undignified way to go," Finch remarked. He didn't bother waiting for her response. He knew on normal occasions she'd burst with fury. Her tantrums were storied. But here, with so many eyes on them both, she'd have to smile and sip her way through it.

"Oh, darling... how terribly brave of you to endure another night of this circus, knowing full well how it always ends for you," she said.

She took a slow, sucking pull on her drink then dabbed the corners of her sloppy lipstick. "If you don't win this year, I just don't know what else you might try, though I hear they're always looking for ushers at the *Rialto*. A man of your skill could certainly wield a flashlight, don't you think?"

"And likewise, Vivian, I'm astonished you're still clinging to ingenue roles like a bat on a cave ceiling. Though I suppose with enough stage powder and grease on the lens, even Tutankhamun could get a close-up," Finch replied.

Horace V. Bellamy sat next to Finch and snorted. *The* Horace V. Bellamy. He'd once taught Finch everything he knew, gave him his first crack at the business. Not to mention he was the bigshot producer at *Regal Monarch Studios*, which headlined the town. Horace tried passing off his choking amusement at Finch's comeback as though a dry bit of cheese had created chaos in his throat.

It was a sparkling evening at *The Majestic Royale Hotel*. *The Palm & Pearl Club* in the hotel's lower bowels was the perfect fanciful setting with its imitation coconut trees, waiters dressed as puffy-sleeved conga players, and cigarette girls with their strappy trays and pillbox hats. It was as if the *Hollywood Extras Syndicate* had sent out a bulletin and filled the place with costumed supernumeraries.

The announcer, in his impeccable tuxedo, stood at the mic and held an envelope high.

"Thank you, ladies and gentlemen, for your dedication to our Guild. And for your participation tonight in honor of the standout members in our industry. We have two categories remaining. Our first is for Best Actress in a leading role. This year's nominees include Ruby Leclair for her role in the sweeping romance, *Midnight Serenade*... June Carlisle for her portrayal of a mysterious woman caught up in a crime in *The Glass Widow*... Isadora Vellani as an exiled Russian aristocrat in *Dark Orchid*... and Vivian Delacroix, who plays an heiress fighting for her marriage through terminal illness in *A Kiss Before Dying*."

The audience offered soft, gloved applause and murmured to one another.

"Our winner tonight is Vivian Delacroix, *A Kiss Before Dying*."

The audience applauded with enthusiasm, and Vivian swooped up onto the stage with a hungry look, as though the statuette was a juicy prime rib she'd been eyeing all year.

Finch felt his pulse throb in his ears, and it seemed as though the room tilted. Best Picture was next. The Guild had overlooked *Storm Over Belle Fontaine* in every other category so far. But he alone would stand for *CineFilm* in that electric moment if they opened an envelope and uttered the name of the film, or rather, Edmond's film.

Belle Fontaine was his pet project. Finch kept him from it for years because he always had other pictures, bigger projects than a sweet, if not sappy, romance. If Belle Fontaine won, it would be Edmond's victory as much as his.

Vivian cackled into that microphone, a villainess draped in feathers and stagecraft. He didn't hear a word of whatever she blabbered. Before long, she'd left the stage with her shimmering prize, leaving Finch at the table with Horace, who withdrew a cigar from his lapel pocket.

"I always like to be prepared. Best of luck, Bramwell. You've done well for yourself, my boy, despite how things turned out," Horace said.

Finch nodded and gave a disinterested smile. Though he would never be able to repeat anything Horace just said to him.

The announcer returned to the mic, envelope in hand.

Finch saw his lips moving. He saw Horace lean in, his eyes gleaming. He knew that the man onstage was reciting names. His name. Someone else's name. It should have mattered.

But Finch's heartbeat thundered in his ears, and his hands clasped so tight, his fingers went numb.

The starry night sky seemed to swallow the room. The chandeliers shimmered above, diamonds caught the light, but none of it felt real. His fingers nabbed at the edges of the tablecloth near his lap. He'd allowed his hands to escape from their clutching. But he shouldn't have. Now they were finger-pulling that cloth and the glasses inch by inch toward him.

Then, applause, a crash of cheers, and the crisp kiss of glass on glass. Horace rose from his chair.

Finch blinked. He'd lost his breath. The starry sky dimmed to nothing. Horace walked toward the stage. The golden statuette was his, not Finch's. Again, close, but not good enough.

He heard his father's voice just as easily as the announcer's. The voice returned, dark and unyielding. "*Go ahead. Cry. That's all you ever did better than anyone else.*" He felt a wave of dizziness. Maybe he was on the floor, like Vivian, fainting away with the back of her hand to her brow.

But no. He was still sitting, heart plummeting.

The room fell silent. He could no longer speak, no longer scream, though that's what he needed.

They all sat still. Words stopped mid-sentence. Champagne bubbles suspended in their glasses, and a waiter stopped mid-pour. A layer of frost seemed to settle into the air. Everyone there was a sheeted body, like those from the morgue at Saint Cyprian's. A thought pierced him, cold and quick. A sharp dagger. *All of them dead*, he mused.

But he let it go.

No one stood at the microphone any longer. There was a lone spotlight casting a dim circle upon the black stage. In the center was the music box from his office. It began to turn, spilling its dainty song into the air and infecting it. *Silent Night.*

He reached for the sheet of the person sitting next to him and pulled it until it rustled away to the floor. It was Vivian. Her face rotting and her skin peeling away. Her eyes were white and staring at the empty stage.

"Vivian," Finch said. "Vivian, the gag's over." He held the martini glass to her discolored lips. "Keep drinking, dear. You're not sufficiently sloshed."

She remained mute and as unmoving as the freezing air. She had no breath. From his own mouth, his breath formed white puffs. But Vivian sat with not a fog, not a flutter. Her eyes, once sharp with contempt, now stared forward, dulled like overfired porcelain.

Finch gave a shaky laugh. "Darling, Horace just won, and you're like a mannequin in the *Bonwit Teller* window. I thought he signed your paychecks."

The glass slipped from his hand and landed between her shoes with a dull, slushy clink. But she didn't rise for her cue. It was as if she'd just paused. It was as if the film they all occupied had jammed in the projector, and now she was breathless, her motions suspended.

And that rot... how in God's name did she get that?

Finch noticed movement from deep in the recesses of the black velvet hanging panels that made the theater wings. Someone lurked there, dressed in white, though the legs were all wrong. They had an odd shape, bent where they shouldn't be. They were too thin at the knee, too thick at the thigh. No, not a thigh... it was something else. And there was a backward joint. A sharp edge caught the low stage light. Hooves. There were hooves.

His eyes trained upward, while whatever words might come next instead lodged in his throat. The figure stood unmoving, watching. Its face was long, unnaturally so, and shadow lengthened beneath high cheekbones. The eyes were wide set. Too wide to be human. They were dark and glinting, and they seemed to peer from either side of its head.

The applause returned in an instant, a crashing wave of noise that knocked Finch back to the moment. His ears rang as Horace strode up to the stage, shook hands, flashed a broad grin, and clutched the gold figurine.

Vivian lifted her martini from across the table and tossed Finch a smirk.

Finch's chest felt tight. The room was now too hot and too bright.

Someone was talking to him, he realized. A waiter? No, a reporter. The flashes had started. The familiar *pah-pah-pah* of cameras sounded off around him.

He was already outside, and the gala was done. So was his career, he mused.

When had he left the table? *The Palm & Pearl*?

He heard a voice. Sharp. Probing. "Mr. Finch, any words on tonight's loss? Is it true that *Storm Over Belle Fontaine* was your last shot at the Guild's highest honor?"

Finch could smell the man. His ugly brown hat, covered in old sweat. And his breath, like he'd eaten garlic all day, and it was rotting in his innards. Finch had a fleeting impulse to grab his pencil and pad and hurl them into the street.

Instead, he smiled. It was the kind meant to play to the crowd.

"You're asking about *my* career? Must be easy to judge from the gutter. And between you and me, you reek of yesterday's bratwurst and today's irrelevance. However, to answer your question: No. It wasn't my last shot. I'll be up there. Upon my grave, I'll be up there. But write what you'd like; you always do. Just remember, ink washes away easier than Bramwell Finch."

THREE

THERE WERE ONLY SECONDS before the train would shred her. He'd tied her hands and feet with rope, and he'd gagged her with a scarf so no one would hear her screams.

Whoooo. She heard it coming around the bend and struggled against the ropes. He'd fastened her down, looping the bindings through the track ties. She'd not find a way out of this.

Whoooo. She felt a cold hum and then vibration along the rails. It didn't matter that she had piles of blonde ringlets cascading down her neck to provide a cushioning layer. Her skull rattled fast, wild, unstoppable, like it might come loose from her spine. The train barreled forward, blind and merciless, churning the air in big hot exhalations.

She bit through the fibers of the scarf that choked her. It loosened around her lips and slipped down her chin. But what help was a freed tongue? A scream of terror to benefit the barrel cactus and the rattlesnakes? No one would come. No one knew. She lay on a track far from a merciful ear. Rescue was unlikely as pistons and gears began to bear down the rails.

All the world was a mechanical roar... and that incessant whistle.

Woooo.

WOOOO.

"No!" she said.

She might as well have whispered it. The Great Northern Liner thundered toward her—263,000 pounds of iron, fire, and steam, raging like blind fury. And she was ninety-three pounds of flesh and panic, left to a grisly end.

Once she was nothing but bits and pieces, he would claim the remainders of her existence. He'd take her home. And as for her child, he'd consign her to some forgotten orphanage. Once she was gone, there was nothing but pillaging. And that he'd do with delight. He wouldn't even blink afterward. He'd just go on to sit for his Christmas dinner.

Dastardly.

Woooo. She heard the steam shoot from the pistons, hissing, sizzling like hot death. Closer it came. *Closer*. She could feel the engine, black and furious, towering as it came just within a few yards. Soon she would feel it at her neck. Her poor child. Her poor child.

"Cut," Victor said.

The word descended like a hatchet, slicing clean through the scene. This take seemed as good as any.

From behind the wooden train cutout, a man with an untucked shirt, suspenders, and a flat cap stepped into view.

A Santa Ana wind whipped through the set, kicking up Mojave dust and toppling the flat, painted train board with a dry clatter. Two stagehands behind it jumped back just in time, still clutching their smoking black pots, used to give the impression of steam.

"Goddammit, Victor, I'm not lying here all day," Scarlett said. "I've headlined three pictures, and I played the national tour of *Frenchie's Feathered Fannies*, you bonehead. I don't need to be out here with scorpions nesting in these cheap ringlets!"

Her voice was all razors, and it landed somewhere near a screech. She stood, shucked off the ropes, and she stalked off in the direction of the dressing trailers. She kept talking, and the crew rolled their eyes for the umpteenth time.

"No one's asking you to, Scarlett," Victor said.

She stopped before she'd exited the set and spun on her heel like the camera was still rolling and the applause was overdue.

"You're to call me *Miss Diamond*," she said. "Got that? I deserve a little respect, after all. And this makes six takes of this lousy train scene. Who *wrote* this hokum anyway? And just who's running this circus? You call us out here on a windy day, and I'm caked in sand and dust. I didn't spend half the day in the makeup trailer just to look like a bride of *The Mummy*."

Just then, the boom mic dangling from above, its operator oblivious, dipped too low and hooked her wig. When he realized what had happened, he pulled on the lever and yanked the fake locks clean off. It tossed high, and then the heap of blonde ringlets hit the ground, looking like a crime scene at a doll factory. Beneath the torn away rent-a-hair lay her own thinning thatch pinned tight beneath a wig-cap.

Scarlett froze. The crew took a collective in-breath. A hush fell over the set.

"Jesus *Christ*, Victor," she said. She snatched up the hairpiece. "Call me when it's no longer amateur hour."

She marched off with her curls bouncing in her fist, and she slammed her trailer door as she entered it.

One of the smoke pots was too close to the train cut out, and it caught fire at one edge. A stagehand blasted it with a hissing fire extinguisher.

Victor ran a hand over his face and sighed.

"Jeez. I'm sorry, Mister Landon." The man behind the train set-piece spoke. "I thought it was going well until the wind knocked it out of my hands. You can't predict when it'll blow. If you want, we can make a sturdier piece... maybe hook it to the front of a wagon."

Victor talked through the fingers covering his face. "No, Joe. We're out of time, and we've already stretched the budget as far as we could. We'll have to make this last take work, and we'll see what we can recover in editing."

"Victor? Come on. Scarlett's right. We already have six takes. I'm not sure how it'd get better. Besides, you shouldn't expect more from them, especially not today," Rosalind said.

Rosalind Crisp was sensible. She kept her wet-set blonde waves in rolls across her scalp. She looked efficient and no-nonsense. She wore round tortoiseshell glasses that enveloped half her face and clutched a clipboard. Just as orderly as a file drawer. She often kept a pen clenched between her teeth in the inevitability of script revisions. She wasn't plain, but she wasn't Scarlett Diamond either.

"You're probably right, Crispy," he said. "I should have known not to expect their best on Christmas Eve day. We'll come back to this and see what we can piece together later. Besides, today's shoot was really all about *tonight*."

"Well, to be safe, we'll keep you-know-who from the dailies, and he'll just assume we kept to our schedule," she replied.

"Do you think word reached Finch about tonight?" he asked.

"Of course not. He was at the Laurels last night, and I'm sure he's spent the day nursing a grudge and drafting a very dramatic memo to *Someone In Charge* while sitting in his enormous, empty mansion."

"Was it that bad?" he asked.

"Bellamy won... again."

"And *Belle Fontaine*?"

Rosalind shook her head. "Oh, it got a nod... but I'm not sure anyone ever watched it from start to finish. Even the *Backlot Bulletin* called it '*Snore* Over Belle Fontaine.' It deserved a little more than that. Didn't you think? Anyway, you can't stop people from whispering.

And the Guild can't afford to be mixed up in scandal. And now, without Malvern around to temper him, he's more Finch than even *he* can take. And he was already a strong cup of coffee. Oh, I'm sure the Guild just *loves* him right now. Malvern used to keep him occupied. But now he's getting involved in every department. He's obsessed with winning one of those awards." She sighed. "Last week, before the ceremony, did you know he actually stalked Heddy Farnsworth?"

"The head of the *Motion Picture Guild*?"

"Now that Edmond is gone, Finch has slipped from the *Toast of Hollywood* to *the Ghost of Hollywood Past*," she said.

"It sounds like opportunity knocking, Rosalind. The man is drowning. Now may be your chance. Remember when you took over for me on the set last month? What I saw in the dailies was perfection. You already have the chops and he knows it. For God's sake, you studied with him under Bellamy at his hand-picked salon. How many years was that? You'd be doing him a favor if you directed one for CineFilm. At least he'd have a chance of winning one of those awards. If he keeps this up, CineFilm's finished. We might as well start sending out résumés."

"Well, I'd be the first to sign up if they started handing out director's chairs to women, wouldn't I? Look, why don't we call this a wrap and get to the *Velvet Derby*? I want a head start just in case Finch can sniff out holiday joy and he hunts it down like it owes him money," she said.

"And you're sure Diamond didn't tell him anything?" Victor asked.

"Everyone's kept her out of the loop. Besides, if Finch already knew, don't you think his springs would have popped by now?" Rosalind raised her eyebrows. "This party is one of the few things going right, and the cast really needs it. Besides, I called him an hour ago. He wouldn't come to the phone, so it looks like we're in the clear. Now, come on. Let's get out of here before he materializes out of sheer resentment."

"You're probably right. Go ahead and call it, Crispy," he said.

Rosalind gripped the white, conical speaking trumpet and aimed it toward the dozens of actors and crew. "That's a wrap, folks! And just a reminder: miss the six o'clock soiree, and don't be surprised if Santa forgets your agent's name next year."

The crowd cheered and set to work dismantling the fictitious railway and hauling away set-piece shrubbery.

"What do we do about Miss Diamond?" Victor asked.

Rosalind squinted. "As far as I'm concerned, she can marinate in her own ego and whatever perfume she uses to fumigate the dressing trailers."

"So, what? We just leave her?"

"Put a note on her door. Leave directions to *The Royal Flush* in Riverside."

A clarinet wailed through a rendition of *Smoke Gets in Your Eyes,* and the small cast and crew huddled at their table candles gossiping, guffawing, smoking, and guzzling from large tumblers of beer and ice-clinked cocktail cups. A skinny Santa in an oversized red suit with a pillow for a stomach stood in a clapboard-cut out sleigh while crooning the song into a chrome microphone.

Just last year, vice might have turned up and hauled everyone off. But in Hollywood, rules bowed to sequins and studio clout. The production companies landed friends in the right places, and the city's elite rarely lacked highballs and giggle water. The police turned a blind eye. Sometimes they even smiled for the flash pots next to studio executives.

Still, in 1934, the aftertaste of Prohibition lingered. There were sermons on the airwaves, watchdogs in the wings, and scandal always ready for its close-up. Rosalind and Victor couldn't risk any surprise press coverage, not when Finch was on perpetual simmer.

Since Malvern died, the whole studio teetered like a wobbly marquee in a windstorm. The Depression, Finch's fraying composure long masked by past success, and a string of recent flops had all piled up like dried kindling. Hushed talk circled the backlot like stagehands in the wings, waiting for the cue to drop the final curtain. Everyone knew that one whisper of impropriety in the columns, one scandalous quote about an unauthorized cocktail party, and CineFilm might go up in smoke. That would mean everyone's jobs.

But December, with its promises of warm fellowship, had a way of dulling such fears. It lured people from caution with spiced air and firelight, with Yule logs and familiar songs, and the strained wish that they might still redeem a tarnished year. For a moment, they forgot the headlines and the unpaid invoices. And nothing fogged judgment faster than cheap bubbly.

Everyone present knew Mister Finch. He would never have approved of such a dining extravagance. Still, the holiday revelers turned to the feast and pretended not to wonder who would pay the price. Only Victor kept glancing toward the lobby, half-expecting Finch to walk in and see exactly where a chunk of the *Runaway Reckoning* budget had gone.

After the feasting and the music, most of them would return to threadbare apartments and uncertain futures. Holiday cheer could only stretch so far, especially in Hollywood, where fortunes and handshake deals changed faster than lighting cues. Even the leads knew they were one flop or scandal away from hoofing it down Sunset.

Rosalind eyed Victor.

"You can relax. I called twenty minutes ago, and he still wouldn't come to the phone. His driver, Samuels, picked up and said he'd be busy for the rest of the day. Every year at this time, Finch goes to Malvern's grave. Probably waiting for a photographer to catch his noble act. Then he's stopping by one of his picture houses, I think the Rialto, and he'll end the day at *Chucky's Steaks* downtown for a porterhouse." She shrugged. "So rest your nerves. He's occupied. If he were coming, he'd be here already. Cane, glare, and all."

"Perverse," Victor replied. "Hard to imagine he marks the date at all, let alone with a steak. Especially knowing how it happened."

"When it comes to Finch, you learn not to ask too many questions," she said. "Especially about that day."

On the other side of the room, one scriptwriter named Shellby, known for his antics and capacity for gin, had assembled a costume consisting of a serving bowl for a hat and a tablecloth for a cape. There was a broom he found in a custodial closet, and he swung it with a flourish that everyone recognized.

"Oh, look, another round of useless notes from these screenwriters," Shellby said. Finch's caricature was not inaccurate. "The only people I know who can take three months to further ruin an idea I hated in the first five seconds."

The others busted up, and it ended in an uproar of guffaws. They lifted Shellby onto the table, and he continued.

"Brilliant. Another draft. At this rate, we'll be perfect right around the time I'm lowered into the grave," Shellby said.

"But sir, it's Christmas Eve. I have nine children," another writer said.

The fake Finch replied, "Fascinating. And yet, much like a finished script, I've never seen proof of one."

The others howled and lapped it all up.

The music cut out. A scatter of gasps followed, then the sharp clatter of a tray full of silverware. Several glasses smashed on the floor, crystal exploding in a tinkling rain across the tiles.

The air seemed to tighten, as if the room itself had drawn breath and forgotten how to exhale. From behind Rosalind and Victor, Finch appeared, red-faced, eyes glinting like steel in the golden wash of the Derby's chandeliers.

Victor almost inhaled his caviar. He pivoted to face Finch, muscles locking one by one like a wind-up doll with a jammed key.

Shellby, still perched on the table in mid-performance, tightened his lips, went paler than the asbestos snow on the floor, and flung off his tablecloth cape. He scrambled down, nearly toppling a silver platter as the others at the table backed away.

The tails of Finch's coat swayed like restless wings as he tapped his cane against the floor, his eyes sweeping the room. Flutes of champagne, heaping plates, and every ounce of excess lay exposed.

From behind him, Scarlett Diamond glided in, wearing a shimmering red silk dress and a matching mink stole that clung to her alabaster shoulders. She smiled and reached out, brushing Finch's cheek with blood-red lacquered nails. He recoiled, as if her touch had left a stain.

"I told you, Finchy. Heard them from my dressing room," she said.

Finch strode forward, his cane clicking like a metronome. "Creamed spinach. Pommes duchesse. Prime rib. A feast fit for royalty. At a price fit for ruin."

He plucked a half-empty wineglass from the tabletop and inspected it under the light.

"You wouldn't happen to know who is footing the bill for all this holiday spirit?"

"I am, sir," Victor said. He sounded like he hadn't had a glass of water in a week.

"That's right, you are." Finch set the glass down and folded a napkin with surgical precision, all the while staring at Victor like an error to be erased. "And I will audit your budget posthaste to be sure there are no discrepancies."

Rosalind clutched Victor's arm and muttered to him, "Victor. Why did you say that? How are you going to...?"

"What's that?" Finch asked, cupping a hand to his ear. "Funds running a bit low? Pity."

He narrowed his eyes. The kill was coming. "Such a disappointment, Victor. And to think I plucked you off that park bench because I believed you still had something left in you. At least loyalty. You know, to make up for the questionable talent. From the look of the dailies on this literal train wreck of a film, it appears you are still about as empty as those scattered whiskey bottles you left behind."

"Now wait a minute," Victor said.

"I'll cover it," Rosalind said.

"But Rosalind..."

She didn't look at Victor. Her eyes were locked on Finch.

Finch met her gaze, held it, then gave a slow, slick smile.

"No need to pass the hat," he said. "The audit will show what needs showing."

He turned back to Victor. "Won't it? And I will expect to see you both in my office tomorrow morning."

"But tomorrow is Christmas," Rosalind said.

Finch gave no reply.

His attention went to Shellby, and with a single, sharp motion, ripped the tablecloth from his hands, sending the nearby platters to the floor.

"And how charming." Finch tilted his head, studying Shellby like a pinned butterfly under a magnifier. "You've been holding out on me. And they said vaudeville was dead. Let's see if your little act plays without a paycheck."

"What do you mean?" Shellby asked.

"Ladies and gentlemen, a quick announcement," Finch said. He turned in place like he was at the Old Globe, delivering lines with fatal precision. "Since you've all had such a delightful time celebrating... presumably on my dime, I thought I'd give you one more reason to remember this Christmas Eve. *Runaway Reckoning* is officially derailed. How do the oysters Rockefeller taste now? There will be no picture. Not tomorrow, not next week. Not ever. Consider this your closing scene: the part where I cut the budget and roll the credits. Feliz Navidad."

The others stiffened in silence.

"But, Finchy, what about me?" Scarlett asked.

"Ah yes. You. Did you think you'd made yourself indispensable? You're as delusional as you are conniving. The reports of your unhinged behaviors on set made it to the wrong ears, Diamond."

"But, but..." she said.

"Perhaps a good use of time now is to pawn that filthy possum-pelt of yours to avoid the breadlines and pray that some unfortunate producer throws you another bone," Finch said.

Scarlett placed a hand upon the paste-diamonds at her throat. They caught no light now and seemed dull as gravel.

Finch let his gaze sweep the room. He savored the silence. The party lay gutted, the laughter gone. Christmas cheer was in pieces. Only then did he turn.

He strode into the cold Christmas void, the Derby's flickering neon lights sputtering like dying breath behind him.

FOUR

VICTOR STEPPED OUTSIDE, SLIPPING an envelope into his coat. "You're a miracle, Rosalind. I'll pay you back. I promise."

She smiled and touched his arm. "Don't think about that. What's most important is for you to slip it back on the books before Finch discovers the party budget and explodes."

"I'll drop it in the bank's night deposit and bury it in a set dressing invoice. My cousin's a genius with mock-ups. No questions asked. Even if Finch starts counting tassels, he won't catch a thing. The budget will look clean, and he can go back to sulking in the projection room, muttering about camera angles," Victor said.

"I'm just glad I could help. It was the least I could do," she said. She looked at him as if memorizing the moment. Then she blinked away, tucked a stray curl behind her ear, and realized she felt warm. Maybe it was the party, the booze, the giddiness of pulling one over on Finch. She wasn't sure of anything anymore... and she knew Victor could see it.

"Oh? And what's the most?" he asked.

He leaned closer.

A hand reached from inside the apartment and swung the door wide. A young man stood there in spectacles and a knitted vest, eyeing the two of them.

"Mother. It's getting a bit late, wouldn't you say?"

"Just a minute, Tim. I'll be right in," she replied.

Tim checked his wristwatch. "Fine. One more minute. But I'm waiting. Right here. On the other side."

He left the door half-open.

"Don't worry, Victor. My son's harmless. Oh, he means well, but he's a bit..."

"Overprotective?" Victor offered.

She smiled and looked down. "I'd like to finish this conversation sometime."

"Same," Victor said.

"I'm still right here," Tim called. "Fifteen... fourteen... thirteen...."

"We'd better call it a night. Merry Christmas, Victor," she said.

"Of course," he replied. Then louder: "And Merry Christmas to you, Tim!"

She watched Victor hurry down the steps and vanish into the night. Tim used his foot to open the door, his hands remaining clasped over his ears.

"It's safe now," Rosalind said.

"Are you sure? I'm already living with my mother. One more trauma, and they'll have a picture of me in a textbook under 'Classic Neurotic Collapse.'"

Rosalind stepped inside, shut the door, then pressed her back against it.

"There was nothing to hear... or see," she said. "Oh, well."

"Mother, I don't know exactly what was going on out there, but I'm pretty sure playing coy isn't something women your age do. Or men, for that matter. He was begging for something more."

"Will you stop? There was nothing going on. I was just lending a friend some money," she said.

"What? The money you stashed?" Tim asked. "I distinctly remember your mother telling me money belongs in sugar tins."

"Settle down, Tim. I only gave what I could. At least it was for a worthy cause," she said.

"I'm a worthy cause! Don't you want me out of the house?"

"I don't know about that..." She walked toward him like a dancer, shoulders back. She threw her arms around his neck. "I think we'll probably have to stick together for now."

"Why are you saying that?" Tim asked, stepping back. "There's something you're not telling me. What happened today?"

Rosalind took a deep breath and wandered across the apartment. She began mixing ingredients she'd set out for Christmas cookies.

"Nothing, really," she said. She cracked some eggs and tossed the shells in the trash.

"If nothing happened, why was that director on our doorstep taking money and *whatnot* from you? You were supposed to still be at that Christmas party at the Derby."

"Can we change the topic?" she asked.

"Then it *is* true," Tim said. "I ran into Ronnie from makeup at the Owl Drugstore, and she said Finch cancelled the picture. But knowing Ronnie and her gossip, I ignored it."

"So it's out, then. Well, let it be. The film's gone, but we're still standing. Finch suspected Victor had reallocated a bit of the budget, and he was right. He hadn't taken it for himself. It was only enough to give the cast and crew a small holiday kindness. And the rest you already know. We made it right, the budget is whole, and nobody's going to jail. Our pockets will be lighter in the meantime. Still, we have each other. That's what counts, right? Each other, and our health. What more could we want on Christmas Eve?"

"Finch... Whatever held him together, it went with Malvern," Tim said.

Rosalind tasted the cookie dough from the spatula.

"They were inseparable, those two," she said. "Used to lock themselves in the screening room every Christmas Eve. I think he still does it, come to think of it."

She gave a quiet laugh, but there was no warmth in it.

"I'm not excusing him. Tonight was brutal. But the look on his face when he walked in... That was a man realizing he wouldn't be missed."

She set the spatula down. "Funny. I looked up to him long ago. Now all I see is a man chasing ghosts—or being chased by them."

Tim's eyes widened at his mother's words. He paused. "Wow. Tidings of comfort and joy...." He brought her to the couch. "Okay, I need you to back away from the cookies before you bake your tears into them. Wait here. I need to get you something that isn't dripping with depression."

He dashed from the room, and Rosalind heard clattering in the other. She kept the conversation going.

"You should've seen Shellby when Finch caught him mid-impersonation. Looked like a schoolboy marched to the blackboard for punishment, and he practically curtsied."

She smiled to herself, but it faded.

"In my next life, maybe I'll run the studio. I'll make the films. I'll be kind. I'll remember people's names and who it was that helped me along the way."

Tim plopped onto the couch with his mother and set down a package wrapped in brown paper and tied with a red ribbon.

"What's this?" Rosalind asked.

"What does it look like?"

"Unless you've wrapped the landlord's patience in red ribbon, I'd say it looks like a problem."

"Mother. Relax. Just enjoy the holiday," Tim said. "Besides, if you really want me to blow our savings, I've got a few wild ideas of my own for how to do it properly."

He kissed her flour-dusted forehead.

"You should have that dream of yours, and you should make your movies," he said.

"No one's hiring a lady director. Not now anyway," she replied.

"The world's not ready for what it just can't understand," Tim replied. "But one day it will. And when that day comes, you'll be right there, and they're going to love you. Now put this gift under the tree, and no peeking until tomorrow morning. Promise?"

"Why are you all dressed up?" she asked. "What are you doing tonight? I thought we were having cookies and humming Christmas carols by the fireplace."

"Hilarious... I'm meeting someone," Tim said.

"Anyone I know?" Rosalind asked. She squinted.

"Nah, she's new. Not sure she's ready for the maternal inquisition just yet," he said.

"Mmm. Christmas Eve... a mystery woman. I suppose miracles still happen," she said.

"Please. I haven't even committed to a Christmas sweater yet," he said. He grabbed his coat from the rack. "Okay. Merry Christmas. Don't wait up."

"See you in the morning... Try not to break too many hearts," she said.

He slipped out the door, and after it shut, she closed her eyes.

"The world isn't ready for what it doesn't understand."

There wasn't a star in the sky that night. Not even the moon. Finch had never seen a darkness like this. It was thick, suffocating, and absolute. A film premiered just down the road, but the searchlights that should have swept the night sky never came. Just blackness.

The few lights still visible were those above the studio gates, spelling out *CineFilm Finch and Malvern Studios*. And even those looked like they struggled to keep from being consumed by the shroud of night.

"Samuels," Finch said. There was no response from his driver.

"Samuels!" He tried again, using the speaking horn near his seat. "Why isn't the gate opening?"

There was more silence.

"Samuels, can you hear me?" Finch stepped out into the inky night, the air chilled with a winter haze that crept across the grounds. He stepped forward and tapped the driver's window with the silver knob of his cane.

Samuels didn't open the window, nor did the door swing wide. That was strange. He couldn't see inside.

He looked across at the guard shack. Benny, who'd never once missed a night in ten years, was gone. The light inside the little booth shivered as Finch stepped closer. Benny wasn't one to leave his post, unless he'd gone to see what was wrong with the power.

Inside the shack, Finch found a paper lunch sack with a half-eaten sandwich. There was a silver flask tucked but peeking from inside a winter coat. He unscrewed the flask and sniffed. Brandy. And it smelled like it could strip paint. Benny likely assumed no one would come by, not on Christmas Eve. Outrageous. Abandoning his post. And *this*.

Finch returned to the limousine and tapped on the glass. Samuels was unresponsive, and Finch wrenched the door open.

"Samuels! When I call for you...."

No one was there.

"What the devil?" Finch said.

Farther up the main drive stood the stairs to his upstairs office. A nearby lamppost cast a sickly gray light over a figure standing below.

"Samuels? Is that you? Benny? What are you doing there?"

The man didn't answer. He didn't move.

"Samuels? Speak, goddammit. Whoever you are, this is private property. You're trespassing."

He paused.

Not a word. Not a step. Just a shadow, watching. Finch's stomach turned.

He tightened his grip on the silver-tipped cane and marched forward past the gates and into the studio backlot.

"Sir. You cannot stand on these grounds. I insist you leave at once!"

Finch watched as the silhouette reached up with both hands and lifted its head from its shoulders. He stopped cold. So did his breath.

The man in shadow let the object drop. It rolled down the winding sidewalk, tracing each curve as if guided by an unseen hand.

"What... what is that?" Finch asked. But no answer came.

It continued down the path then bumped off the curb to the asphalt, making soft, wet sounds like a spongy bowling ball. It rolled to a stop at Finch's feet.

He pulled his spectacles from his vest pocket and slid them on.

Staring up at him was Malvern's severed head.

It watched him with frightened eyes and rotting features. To Finch's astonishment, the mouth dropped open. It was not slack with death, but it moved with intent. Cinders spilled from his mouth, glowing like hot coals, orange and red, then crumbling into dust across the pavement.

Once the mouth had emptied, a gasp of a word escaped its lips. "Fiiinch."

His chest clutched tight, and a cold surge flooded his limbs. He reeled, his legs giving way beneath him, and he dropped to the pavement.

"God in heaven," Finch said. Though it came out closer to a strangled whisper.

He scrambled backward in a surge of electric fear, making sounds he didn't recognize as human. Then he raised his cane like a weapon.

He glanced toward the lamppost.

The headless figure that had stood there was gone, leaving only the trembling light behind.

There was no severed head at his feet, either. In its place, a skunk waddled past his spats.

Finch raised his cane once more then thought better of it.

He brushed himself off, muttering under his breath.

"Malvern... of all things. He's gone. All gone. A head's got nothing to say once it's been unseated...."

The skunk vanished behind the sound stages. Finch stood a moment longer, gripping his cane, staring at the spot where he imagined Malvern's head had spoken his name.

He couldn't explain it. Couldn't explain where Benny had gone. Or Samuels. Or the choking darkness that followed him. He couldn't explain *any* of it, except for being overtired and over-hungry. He hadn't made it to Chucky's Steaks for his annual porterhouse. The Derby spectacle took care of his appetite.

He wouldn't go home.

But he wouldn't tell anyone what he saw, either. All of it was nothing more than some fevered melodrama playing at a cheap matinee. A child's ghost story with a B-list budget.

He still had ledgers to sort through on *Runaway Reckoning*. That's what he told Victor. And that's what he would do. He'd work through the night. He needed the numbers. The accounts due and receivable. Receipts from vendors. Things that added up. Things he could prove.

He returned his gaze to the walkway and the stairs leading to his suite. The lamppost light glowed red. He adjusted his spectacles and leaned forward. The bulb had no tint and never did. Instead, the glass enclosure filled with a red liquid.

"I don't believe it," he said. Then he shouted at the empty surroundings. "Do you hear me? I don't believe it!"

The lamp continued to fill, and the glass burst, splattering the liquid across his new white shirt, staining it with a dark, cold, and unsettling fluid.

Blood. But it couldn't be. It was some substance that looked like it. *No*, he thought. *Not blood. Not blood. In the same splatter. In the very same splatter. But how?*

With the lamp extinguished, the limousine headlights were the only light left. They stretched across the wet pavement, twisting shadows into long, spindled shapes. Bare tree limbs reached out like crooked twig fingers. The building's architecture mimicked a horror-stricken face, lit from below as if caught in harsh theater footlights.

Finch clutched his cane. His breath caught; his mouth turned dry. His heart thudded louder and harder than footsteps in a silent theater.

He shut his eyes and swallowed. He willed his fingers to unclench.

Just get into your office.

Just get into your damn office.

But panic bloomed in his chest. It spread, slow and crawling. It felt like a fracture running through glass, spidering outward and cracking his logic to pieces.

His feet wouldn't move. They couldn't.

No. He would not allow such weakness of mind to dictate his path.

"No need to panic, old boy," Finch said. But even the sound of his own voice failed to reassure him. Words were a poor shield against whatever hallucinations he'd conjured.

He turned instead. The car was closer than the office. He wouldn't have to pass the landscape that bent toward him like claws. Better to wait for Samuels in the confines and safety of the back seat.

But the limousine had lost its familiar shape. It was now a hearse, long and somber, its rear windows drawn over by heavy, scalloping drapes. He squinted and tilted his head, as if a new angle might correct what he saw, and a knot of old dread pulled taut inside him. It felt like an icy wind had blown through his chest. And he felt it was meant for him alone.

Another illusion in the darkness. Perhaps he was ill. Yes. He was likely in his bed at this very moment, twisting in the sheets. One thing could never become another. Heads didn't roll down the walkway. Bushes didn't become clutching creatures. And limousines never changed form. *Preposterous.*

The hearse rumbled to life, and he stood near enough that he felt the purr of the motor reverberate through his limbs.

"Ah, Samuels. I was beginning to think..."

Before Finch could say more, the hearse lurched forward, chirping tires on the asphalt. It broke through the striped barrier-arm and screamed up the drive toward him.

"Samuels!" Finch said.

He didn't care anymore about negotiating the subtleties of delusions. Instead, he sprinted to the staircase and bounded up to the small landing in front of his office door. He was a man of fifty, but he had strength in those bones, more than an onlooker might suppose.

At the top, he leaned forward over the railing and watched the hearse ram through and demolish the staircase, shattering it into planks and splinters. All that remained was Finch's small landing. And brackets only kept that in place. The flooring beneath him squealed under his weight.

The hearse engine cut out and went dark.

"Samuels! Are you insane?"

The back doors of the vehicle opened without a hand reaching for them.

Finch decided he'd not wait another moment to see what might come of it. Hallucination or not, he was not about to stand there gaping to see what might crawl out. He withdrew several keys with his trembling fingers. Without him ever inserting a key into the lock, the door creaked open to a deathly darkened room.

Finch flicked the lights on and off, but they refused to comply. He pulled a pearl lighter from his pocket. The flint sparked. A small flame caught and held.

"I'll call the police. Have that lunatic Samuels arrested. That's what I'll do," he said.

He hadn't stopped grumbling in the dark, and he wasn't sure he ever would. The sound of his voice steadied him, kept his thoughts in facts instead of fantasies.

In his secret heart, he worried that if he went quiet, the dark might answer.

He stumbled through his office by the flicker of his lighter, making his way to the desk telephone. In the faint glow, he caught the outline of a figure standing deep in the room.

The light hissed out.

The shadow remained, an island of darkness in a still, midnight lake.

He felt eyes upon him.

"Who's there?"

He tried the lighter, but it became stubborn and uncooperative. The shadow did not stir. Finch stared back at it and tried to sharpen his gaze to penetrate the gloom.

"Rosalind? Is that you? For God's sake, turn on the lights. Did you see that? Rosalind!"

He squinted into the dark.

"Well, say something. Stop gawking like a tongue-clipped dimwit. You saw Samuels, didn't you? Victor put him up to it. Thinks he can frighten me into backing down."

He took a step forward.

"Well, I'm not a moon-eyed simpleton. You can tell Victor that. I know what he's up to, and it won't work."

Unmoved, the shadow lingered in the stillness of Finch's silences. Finch worked the lighter again. A breeze picked up and slammed the office door. It shut out the world, leaving Finch in a darkness known only by the inside of a casket. The air grew heavy.

The dark watched.

He felt it the way an animal knows it is being hunted; not through logic, but through feeling a gaze that brushes the skin without touch.

Finch lurched forward and bent over his desk, knees knocking against wood. He fumbled with the items there: a stapler, a letter opener, a few manuscripts. The phone had been within reach earlier. It was right there. In plain sight.

His fingers scrambled across the surface. His heart followed, quick and frantic, warning him he might not get out of this.

Whoever was there continued watching. It waited in the blackness, unspeaking.

He leaned one last time across the desk, which seemed to stretch farther with each scrambling sweep of his arms. Then, there. He gripped the receiver and let out a breath. Clicking down on the holder several times to reach the operator. And then the police.

"Hello. Hello?"

Static greeted him. A busy signal followed.

"Fiiinch." The voice sounded at first like wind dragging across the door frame. But then he realized it was the fragile tone of a child. It was a voice that he knew once. It had come searching for him through time.

"Stop this at once, Victor. If anything happens to me, there are witnesses from the party. You won't get away with this."

He heard the wind again, or the voice riding in on it.

"Fiinch."

The voice drifted across the room, slipping from one shadow to another. Then it came to rest in the interior of his private bathroom.

He flicked his lighter, and this time it lit. A weak tongue of fire danced in the otherwise lightless air. The shadow he thought was Rosalind standing in the depths was only his coat rack.

Still, he reached forward and jiggled the bathroom doorknob, but it held fast as though someone on the other side kept him from turning it.

Then a series of booming thuds echoed from behind the closed door. They knocked the breath from him, and he stumbled backward, landing in the seat of a high-backed armchair that he'd recalled as a boy. Yes, it was a fixture in his parents' home, up in the Catskills. The doily protecting the headrest still smelled like his mother.

"Come out this instant! You hear me, Victor? Now, I'll let it all pass as a practical joke, and I won't press charges if you come out this instant. Show yourself, goddammit!"

"Let me out," the child said. "I know you can hear me. No. No! Let me out!"

Yes. Finch knew that voice. He'd heard that cry before. Once when he was afraid to do more than watch and feel his feet turn to ice.

The bathroom door clicked with a rusty clink, and it squeaked open.

Beyond the door was a long, narrow room with a small window at the far end. The panes that opened outward knocked together in the breeze.

He sighed, ashamed of how carried away he'd gotten.

Convinced now it had only been the wind, he stepped into the confining darkness with the smallest scrap of resolve. It hadn't hardened, but it would do. He latched the window shut.

But the old feeling returned and nagged him. He could feel *it* behind him.

A small, tinkling tune played from behind the shower curtain, sending a jolt through his body. *Silent Night* plinked and echoed against the tiles like a carousel tune from an abandoned country fair.

With a sudden yank, he tore the curtain back and brought his raised cane down hard. The silver head struck the tile. Shards scattered across the floor in a rain of dust and splinters.

There it was, nestled in the rubble, sitting in the tub. A Christmas snow globe. Father Christmas stood inside, making a slow turn, then he stopped.

Impossible. It couldn't be here... unless someone had moved it. Lola. Was this *her* doing, with all that nonsense about a grandmother's curse?

At the far end of the shower, a child in knickers and a flat cap shifted in the deep shadows. Finch yelped and stumbled back.

The boy shrank into the corner and turned his face to the wall.

Finch steadied himself. His lungs flexed then shrank. He couldn't remember the last time he'd taken a full breath.

"Who the devil are you? How did you get in here?" Finch asked. He jerked upright, his posture rigid.

The child turned. A beam from the narrow window touched his face, his features skewed by the patchy glow. Finch reached for the lighter and sparked it back to life.

The boy stood mute, shivering as he wept.

In the fitful light, Finch narrowed his eyes. The child looked injured. Burned.

He was narrow in the shoulders and thin-limbed, dressed in clothes from another time. A deep blue velvet jacket with a lace collar.

"Speak up..." Finch said. His voice cracked, unrecognizable, like a man nearing the asylum. "This is trespassing."

His father's voice had crept in, disguised as his own. The tone was the same. It twisted his stomach to hear it aloud, to know it had taken root in him. When had that begun? How long had it been there, lying in wait?

The boy keened, producing a low, doleful sound, like a funeral wail.

Finch reached for the boy's shoulder and brought the lighter flame closer to his face. The child was nothing but a burned mass of flesh, twisted and crisped by fire.

"Jesus Christ." He slammed against the wall behind him and closed his eyes.

"Mister Finch?" Tim's voice came as a gentle note. "Are you all right?"

Finch opened his eyes. His face had contorted into a scream. But he was not where he thought he stood. Instead, he was sitting in the tufted leather chair behind his desk.

"I... what's going on?" Finch asked.

"Sir? Are you all right?"

"I... of course I am."

"Is this a bad time? You told me to meet you. Tonight, remember?" Tim said. "We were talking, but you suddenly started saying something about trespassing. It sounded like you meant someone else was here."

"Someone else...? Yes. You didn't see anyone? A child?" Finch stopped himself. He knew how that would sound.

"A child? No, sir. We were talking about the script."

"Script?"

"Yes, sir. I gave my mother the script tonight. You know, the one you gave me with her name on it as director? I did everything you asked. I scrounged up those boxes of photos and programs of Lola. You said you'd call me if they proved to be real. I guess he must have been surprised to see all of those collectables. Anyway, you called me, and I'm here to pick up the rest of what you owe me, just like we agreed on."

Finch glanced around the room. His eyes had a far-off look. He searched the room with his gaze, as if expecting the walls to shift again.

"Yes. Of course," he said. He cleared his throat. "I'm sorry. I'm not feeling too well."

"You're not going back on your word, are you?" Tim asked.

"Going back on my...? No. Of course not," Finch said. He felt rewound. Played back. One frame out of sync.

Tim tilted his head and tried to act as if everything was fine. "Are you wanting a... a *cigarette,* sir?"

"Cigarette?" Finch asked. He looked at his hand holding the lighter, and he lifted his thumb. The flame snapped out of sight.

"I.... No, no cigarette... You mean to tell me you never saw that boy? The one with... there was something wrong with his face...?"

"Sir, I... no. Someone was here? After hours like this?" Tim looked around from his seat. He whispered. "Should you call the police?"

Finch pressed his palms against the leather arms of the chair, as if bracing against a world he no longer trusted.

He rose from his seat and wandered into the bathroom. He slid back the shower curtain. There was no musical snow globe or child. The tiles were undisturbed.

"How did you get up here?" Finch asked. "To my office...?"

"Streetcar. Like *always.*"

"No. I mean. The staircase. How ever did you make it up to the landing?"

Tim crinkled his brow.

Finch strode to the office door and flung it wide. The stairs were there, intact as always. The gate remained lowered and unbroken; the lamp remained whole, and the light burned with its usual amber warmth.

"Mister Finch, I don't know what's going on, but can I just get the money you promised and skedaddle?" Tim asked. "It is Christmas Eve, and I have plans."

"How long have you... how long have you been here... in my office?" Finch asked.

Tim looked at the wall clock. "Well, it's nearing midnight. I'd say ten minutes," he replied.

"*What*? Nearing *midnight*? I arrived at six thirty... how could...?" Finch asked. He returned to his desk and sat in his black tufted chair. There was enough brandy in his crystal decanter to assuage his nerves, and he poured for himself with an unsteady hand.

"You really don't remember?" Tim asked. "I came in and brought that package up against your door...?"

Finch drank one, then another, and set the brandy snifter down. He glanced at the package on the side of his desk, already opened and unwrapped.

Inside was a dark suit. The one Malvern wore. The jacket pocket still bore his monogram, *E.M.*. The county morgue incinerated him while he wore it. But here it was again.

There was a note resting on top of it. Finch unlocked the top drawer of his desk and stuffed it there, clicking the lock back in place.

"Oh, yeah, that note was tied down with string on top. I didn't read it or anything," Tim said.

Finch stared off at the front door then back at the bathroom.

"So... can I have the check? You already made it out..." Tim said.

Finch looked down. His checkbook was open, the pen beside it. His own signature stared back at him as though belonging to a man who remembered things.

"I... already... yes, of course I did," he said.

He tore out the check and handed it with a quivering hand to Tim.

Tim stood and made his way to the door. "And Merry Christmas, Mister Finch. You won't regret this decision."

But before Finch could reply, Tim slipped out the door, and the intercom switch lit up on his desk.

Its buzzing made Finch catch his breath.

"Wait! Come back," Finch said.

He stood and rushed to the door and ripped it open, ready to shout for the young man. But he was already gone. The stairs and balcony were gone again, too. They lay in a heap of splinters and broken lumber one story below. The gate had returned to its broken state, and the walkway lamp continued oozing thick red that poured down the lamppost and pooled like syrup on the ground.

Finch slammed the door and put his back to it.

The intercom buzzed again. The red light held steady, unblinking, waiting for his response.

He shut his eyes against it all, willing the grating sound to stop. Wishing these inconsistencies in time, in place, in *fact,* would end.

It buzzed again, sharper this time. Unrelenting. He could bear it no longer. With his heartbeat in his throat, he returned to his desk. He depressed the speaking switch.

"Who's there?"

FIVE

"SCREENING ROOM SIX."

The voice crackled and sputtered, as though it were a transmission from the moon.

Who was behind this? Victor, maybe. But no, it had to be those writers. He'd seen their faces when they thought he wasn't watching. Heard their laughter. They'd shown their true colors when they were sure he wouldn't catch them.

This... this was their idea. A last laugh with a haunted suit and a bit of gallows theater. Forget writing a Laurel-winner for CineFilm. No. All they wanted now was payback.

Finch's jaw clenched. His gut tightened.

He wouldn't let them win. He'd never let them on the lot again. Shred their reputations with the other studios and then leave them to the breadlines.

But he'd rise again. He'd win.

The intercom hummed and crackled. He pressed the button to speak.

"Who's this?" Finch held his voice steady.

Static was his answer. But somewhere in the audio's background-snow came that tinkling music. *Silent Night*. The snow globe music box.

"Who's there? I'm warning you... this is the last prank of your career. I'll call the police and have you put away."

"Screening Room *Six*." The voice wavered, caught in a wash of hissing and sputtering. Finch recognized the tenor sound. It was a man's voice.

The lights dimmed, as though a power surge had drained the building's life for a moment. The entire room buzzed under some unseen strain.

This was the price for shutting down the film.

The truth was, *Runaway Reckoning* was unfit for a week at a nickelodeon. He'd seen the dailies, and it was a clunker so lifeless, it should've come with a toe tag. He had planned to scrap it regardless.

The Derby debacle was the final straw. That underhanded soiree gifted him with the excuse he needed to swing the axe he'd been holding for weeks. And hiring Victor? That was charity.

The famous Victor G. Landon, once a Laurel darling, hadn't directed since being banned from *Imperial Pictures.* He'd passed out one day, mid-shoot, reeking of absinthe. Finch found him a year later, half-pickled and feeding pigeons from a park bench. He offered him a rope: four tight B-pictures a year, dry as a bone, no questions asked.

For a while, Victor delivered. But *Runaway Reckoning* was different. Finch had entrusted him with Edmond's final script. It wasn't his best, but serviceable enough in skilled hands. Victor might've scraped a Laurel out of it. But from what Finch saw in the screening room, Victor's spark had sputtered out. Whatever talent he once had must've dried up when he dried out. And now he had hitched CineFilm to a bomb. A very expensive one.

Finch used a second stairwell on the opposite side of the building to make his way down to the pavement. The screening rooms required a short walk, but now that it was midnight, a dense fog had rolled into the back lot. It curled around the lampposts and swallowed the pavement ahead, softening the outlines of every building.

Finch grumbled and fussed as he made his way. He used his cane as would someone without sight, tapping along in front of him to be sure he wasn't stepping off a curb, or heaven forbid, he'd turned the wrong way from the stairs and headed out into the Boulevard.

Whispers shifted through the mist, voices murmuring in a tumble of sound Finch couldn't quite make out. But they began to clarify with each step.

"Use your head. Christ, you are the stupidest child." The words landed like a slap: sharp, sudden, and unforgiving.

"Who's there?" he asked. He swung his cane at the dark, striking air.

"He's a hunter... through and through," another said. He knew her voice, but it couldn't be.

"Nathaniel Nathaniel soft and meek, walks with a wiggle and pink on his cheek..."

Then came the cries. The same ones he'd heard behind the bathroom door.

"Let me out! Oh, God. Help me!"

"Who's there? Answer me!" Finch said.

He swatted at the air with his cane, and it struck a surface hard enough to sound across the lot.

He reached and felt it was the corrugated tin of the Quonset huts erected at the lot's outskirts.

"Screening Room Six," Finch said. He laughed, short and sharp.

There was no screening room number six. Even in their finest hour, CineFilm needed no more than three. If this was Victor's doing, if he thought this could salvage anything, then the man was farther gone than Finch realized. Finch rapped once against the Quonset door. The sound cracked too loud against the lonely night.

"No wonder you wound up feeding pigeons in the park," he said. "If you think this passes for suspense, your brain's still sopping in turpentine."

The light above the door buzzed, as though it had taken on more current than it could hold. It flared white-hot. Then the bulb popped.

Just before it burst, Finch saw the number six. Clear. Painted above the door.

"Charming," he said. "But you'll need more than a faulty bulb and a stencil to get under my skin."

He raised his voice loud enough to carry. If anyone was listening, they'd know he was unafraid. And if there weren't others? Then his voice served as an exorcism that might push back at whatever caused unseen voices.

He unlocked the door and stepped through the editing facilities. Everything was just as he'd left it. He had designed the building himself. Edits went straight to the reel, then to preview.

At the entrance to the screening theater, he flicked the wall switch. Nothing. The lights refused to answer.

He stood for a moment, waiting for the lights to blink back to life. They didn't.

"Of course," he said.

Someone had positioned a reel-to-reel projector at the center of the room, between the red velvet chairs. A film reel sat in place, already threaded through the apparatus. It clicked and ticked to life on its own. There was no hand or operator behind it, just light and sound where there should be silence.

Finch said nothing. For once, his mind stilled.

The film sputtered and scratched. Strange markings flickered in the leader, quick and unfamiliar. These were not the usual countdown numbers.

They passed in rapid succession: a symbol inked in curling script, almost religious. Red liquid bubbling between microscope slides. A child's face, mouth wide in a silent scream. A shotgun. A white goat with four horns and a blood-stained mouth.

The film then came into focus, and the projector clicked along. It was the stage at The Palm & Pearl Club. Yes. And they were all seated together. Horace. Vivian. Victor, Rosalind, and her boy Tim. All of them were there. An announcer in a black tuxedo emerged from the side and carried an envelope.

"Thank you for your patience, ladies and gentlemen. And now, on to our final Laurel Award for Best Picture of 1934. One of our entries is the most unusual we've seen. It is a new, mysterious film that promises to raise questions about the very fabric of time and memory. This film dares to ask the question: what earns redemption? And what does it mean to be saved?"

The announcer turned and looked out at Finch. He remained motionless, envelope in hand.

"Tricks and lies. Dime-store drama." Finch flung the words across the room, just in case someone was hiding, snickering at him.

Finch glanced back at the screen, and he saw himself there, standing in his own screening room. In that moment, he felt as though the floor beneath him dropped away. His heart had no weight, no substance.

Finch heard a response. "Oh, Bramwell..."

Finch turned back toward the voice behind him. It seemed to speak from beyond the blinding projection light. But there was no outline, no shadow, no shape. There was only a familiar voice, lingering in the stale air.

"Victor. You ungrateful lush. This is the end of your career. Do you hear me?"

He paused. The reel behind him whirred louder.

"Victor. You ungrateful lush. This is the end of your career. Do you hear me?"

He turned back to the screen and saw his image there, red-faced, cane in hand, shouting into the dark, back at himself who stood in the actual screening room.

The disembodied voice behind him continued. "Look at you, Bramwell. Five years gone, and you're still here. Still shouting into the dark. Still alone. Nothing but that cane and your rage to keep you warm."

"Enough! Turn that film off," Finch said.

He rushed through the empty seats to where he heard the voice, but the room remained as empty as a mausoleum.

"You made promises and broke them. Took their dreams, rewrote endings to suit yourself. Pushed others aside for applause and profit. Now you sit in the dark, unloved, no one left to listen to the lies but you...." the voice said.

Finch hobbled back through the empty rows to the wall telephone near the door. He picked up the receiver and depressed the switch hook several times.

"Hello? Operator? Get me the police."

"You have one chance. Your reel hasn't reached the end, not yet." The voice now came from the phone.

"Damn you, Victor!"

"Bramwell, how do you not know my voice? You've heard it more than a thousand times in this very theater. *Bramwell*, it's me. Look here and see...."

Finch tried to ignore it. It had to be someone else. Anyone else. It was all a filthy fabrication. It was impossible. "It's not true. There's no such thing...."

"Once you're dead, you're dead. We used to say that, didn't we?" said the familiar voice.

"Malvern?" Finch asked. He scanned the room. It was still empty.

"Edmond....?" Finch corrected himself, but the name, the word almost coagulated in his throat.

"Come closer. Look at what you've made," the voice said. But now it came from the screen.

Finch turned and saw his old partner, a projected image, crackling along with the unedited sound. Malvern was dressed as the master of ceremonies on stage at the Palm & Pearl Club. He wore the suit Finch had received in his office, the monogrammed one Tim brought. The one he wore while being cremated.

He looked as he did in life: strong-jawed, blond as summer. But bone showed through his exposed neck, which was sliced from one edge to the other.

Finch fumbled with spectacles he extracted from his vest pocket and saw Edmond's eye sockets, dark and cavernous. The man smiled on the screen and, doing so, the flesh peeled away from his mouth. It splatted to the ground, not in the film, but on Finch's screening room floor.

Finch approached the chunk while holding his glasses at the tip of his nose. His heart jack hammered against his ribs. He swallowed back bile and forced himself not to run.

"Dear God..."

"God has nothing to do with this," Edmond said.

"How...?" Finch asked. He blinked at his partner flickering upon the screen.

"So many opportunities wasted. So many hearts pushed away. And in the end, what have you left but a crumbling façade? A few buildings named after you, only to be torn down before the ink on your obituary dries," Malvern said.

"I'll play along. Fine. There were no opportunities unexploited, *Edmond*. If indeed you are Edmond. And if you've come to regret what we built, then I suppose death has done more than strip your flesh. It's dulled your mind," Finch said.

"Where you saw opportunity," he replied, "there was no more than a grave you dug each day. Instead of a shovel, you dug with lying smiles. Instead of a pickaxe, you cracked lives with unkept promises and with deals inked in despair. Waste. Waste!"

"I see nothing wrong with wringing from the world what it would have otherwise wrung from me. Is that not the way of things, Edmond? Or whoever you are, playing at Edmond? I did not invent the dollar nor how to earn it. I simply learned to play the game well. And *Edmond* learned to play just as well, sometimes better than I. If you've found regret in that, I am sorry for you," Finch replied.

"You wove your webs, Bramwell. Promises, pressure, praise. And always someone else left tangled. You never built, only fed. That's always been your gift: sinking your teeth in and smiling while they bled.

"Now you'll rot, too. Not from death, but from knowing. Knowing what you lost. Watching it slip, frame by frame, through the reel. There are worse things than ghosts, Bramwell. Far worse. Like the thirst for what you never had the courage to reach for," Edmond said.

"I won't stand for this any longer. Stop playing at this charade. Poppycock. Why, you're more cinema than cemetery, whatever you are," Finch replied.

The film looked as though it snagged and began wobbling on the screen. The setting around Edmond warped and became unfocused. The film strip showed sprocket holes, and from its flickering border emerged Edmond's shambling body. He stepped through the screen and down to the floor below.

"What in God's name?" Finch asked. "You stay back. Whatever you are... You stay back, you hear me?"

His jaw quivered, and his tongue ran dry. He tried the door again, this time shoving his shoulder into it. Near the door was an axe behind a small glass compartment for fires.

Edmond drifted forward, his arms outstretched to take Finch.

Finch broke the compartment glass with his silver-tipped cane and wielded the fire axe. He chopped at the door and got a hole through to the outside. Edmond approached, his limbs wobbly from death and decay. Finch placed his mouth to the hole he'd made and screamed.

"Help me! Someone, help me!"

He felt a cold hand on his shoulder, and he whipped around, pressing his back against the door. He held the axe in both hands above his head.

"Get away," Finch said. "Or I'll do it. So help me."

Edmond looked on, empty-eyed, unmoved.

Finch brought it down into Edmond's chest. It cracked, and a cloud of black crematory soot engulfed Finch's face.

Finch crumpled to a cowering heap on the floor and hid his face in his hands.

"Why don't you stop? Haven't you had your fill? You've struck terror. Isn't that enough?"

His words came halting between vocal tremors.

"This isn't about terror. It's mercy," Edmond said. He had no lower jaw, and his tongue worked hard to compensate for the lack of lips.

"Mercy—?" Finch asked.

"Yes, for the world, a kindness due. I came to open the way, to deliver hope to all," Edmond said.

Finch coughed on the funereal ash that tainted each of Edmond's words. He gazed upward into his partner's face, remembering when those eyes held something more, something warm, alive. Now they were pits of decay and loss.

"What do you mean?" Finch asked.

"You are not alone, Bramwell. Nor have you ever been," Edmond said.

He twisted his head, and Finch heard the bone fragments crack against one another. More skin flopped away to the floor.

"They follow you... Those confined to the darkness. Shadows, full of craving. You've felt them, haven't you? Wandering the hallways of your soul. Regret... all of it made at your own hands. Each of these hungers for your flesh and will lap at the corruption in your soul, and I cannot stop them. They will not remain hidden this night. Whether you want them, they will come. They will show you. Teach you, if they can. Pry at the vault of your heart that you've sealed so tight. And if it will not loosen, they will take what is theirs."

"*Shadows*? What do you mean they'll take...?"

"Each will come as they are needed."

"I'd rather they not," Finch said.

"Bramwell!" Edmond said. He moaned the last letter of Finch's name and stretched his dry, elongated tongue so it neared entering Finch's own mouth.

Finch squeezed his eyes shut.

"How many chances have you had, *brother*? How many times could you have turned from a ruinous path? *Whether you want, they will come*. They will lay the truth bare. And at the end of it? Justice. Truth. The end of things."

"But Edmond... you above all should understand, if you are indeed a spirit and can see across the planes of time. There were no choices.

Not for me. Not for you. The path was laid, and the stones set upon it, and we walked it because what else was there? Tell me, where were these chances you speak of? If I was blind to such doors when they were open, how could I have changed course? How could I have done anything more than...?"

Before Finch could finish, there was a chime ringing from outside the building.

One o'clock.

He felt a chill, and the air was gray and pale all around him. He saw Edmond standing near the exit in the back rows. But Finch stood elsewhere now. The projector clicked away, and the sound was distant now, faded like a long-ago memory. Its tick-tick-ticking rasped like an echo from another room, another time, just out of reach.

It was as though the sounds had become echoes from another place he'd known once, but not so much anymore.

Six

THE BOY WAS BURNT beyond recognition. All that remained of the child that Finch might discern were two rows of teeth clenched together, the lips singed into charred crisps that outlined them. In his blackened clothing, the child stood, a little tie—or what remained of it—at his throat. Knickers, and what were once shiny leather shoes. Whatever fire had consumed the small being had scorched a piece of his cheek off, and his blackened molars peeked through.

Finch stood facing the small, charred body in a long hallway, and he tried to suppress the nausea he felt looking at the boy in his fire-blistered state. Instead, he turned his attention to the ceilings, which soared above, doming over him like a scrollwork sky. He knew this place.

There was a double door at the end with inlaid wood of several shades. Lights flanked the hall, and they began buzzing and dimming as he strolled past them with the child. They moved in perfect unison, like birds in a twilight murmuration.

"Where am I?" Finch asked. He tried not to look at the boy, or his sickness would persist.

The ash-skinned child pointed, and a wisp of smoke arose from his finger.

"What's behind there?" he asked.

The boy pointed again then stood somber, mute as old oak. Finch reached for the cold brass knob and opened it.

The air was earthy and dusty, filled with the smells of old books. Rows and rows of shelves lined one side of the room. Tall arching windows lined the other, and through them, a misty gray light filtered through, landing with a softness on the room lined with tables, each equipped with a small electric lamp.

A pendulum clock on the far wall marked time with its soft, measured metronome, and a bespectacled woman with lipstick seeping into the crags of her lips staffed a dais in the center.

Still, the child watched Finch with its gelatinous mess of eyes without saying a word.

Finch despised being watched, and now his heart knocked hard. But it was only a child. A bit overcooked, but a child, nonetheless. The floor felt unreliable, and he realized his legs had weakened. He tried to anchor himself with the table, but the room continued to sway.

One might suspect there was no need for Finch to fluster so. He knew this place. And he knew the people in it.

The small presence with his charred little hat and matted clumps of scorched hair continued staring with his black-goo-filled sockets. And he allowed silence to speak.

"You... you are... hurt. You need a doctor," Finch said. "How is it that you stand?"

The small body raised a charcoal hand and pointed to whatever was behind Finch. A small slab of scorched flesh curled upward on his arm.

"Are you...? Are you a shadow of whom Edmond spoke?"

The boy stood, wheezing like an old factory pipe.

"Why have you come for me? Have you not the courtesy to provide an explanation? Why have you brought me here?" Finch demanded.

The boy's silence thickened in the air. He heard himself now, sharp and biting, more than he had thought. His tense demands seemed born of wounds left unhealed. The child's silence outlined his words and threw them into stark relief, exposing Finch to what he dreaded lay beyond.

When he understood the boy would remain a ruined mannequin, Finch gave a resigned sigh and turned to survey the room for clues. *If these shadows dare expect change, they'll have to offer a bit more than silent theatrics,* Finch thought. Even these thoughts, he realized, rose from wounds beyond his reach, buried in the past and left to fester.

He brushed the thoughts aside and spotted a young man at the far end of the library, scribbling with such fervor it seemed the pen had a will of its own.

Finch narrowed his eyes and stepped forward, the edges of the scene sharpening into what he knew would become unbearable. He felt his heart stop for a breath. Years blurred, yet he knew that young man's face.

"I know him," Finch said. "I know him. How can this be?"

The boy no longer stood by Finch, but from the far side of the room he pointed with his blackened hand. Finch returned his gaze to the writer at the desk. A young woman, sensible and smart, tortoise-shell glasses, a bow in her cascading curls and one of them tucked behind her ear, approached.

"Ah, you've come back," the young man said. "I thought you might have gone home. It is Christmas Eve, after all."

She placed two cups and saucers on the young man's writing desk.

"I knew you'd be here, stubborn as always. Even Santa has a little help, you know," she said with a sly grin. "This coffee's boiled so strong, it'll write the script for you. Heck it might even sell the tickets."

"Okay, help me here. Which line sounds more like *Vivian Delacroix*?" He cleared his throat and used his pencil like a cigarette holder. 'Darling, I never stab people in the back. It ruins the line of the dress.' Or how about: 'I never stab people in the back. I have staff for that.'"

"Why are you writing lines for *her*? I thought she was yesterday's news and only good for wrapping fish," Rosalind said. "Anyway, fat chance you'll ever write lines for someone like that... I hear she keeps her underlings in stalls and only lets them out to powder her ego."

She sipped her coffee then gasped. She grabbed him by the shoulders and looked at him as though she'd been struck by genius.

"Hey! Why don't we go down to *Schwimmer's* and get malted milkshakes? It's Christmas Eve, and someone ought to show this town how it's done."

Finch watched Edmond laugh as his hand drifted toward his coat pocket, fingers brushing the small velvet box.

He remembered that. The ring.

Finch and Edmond were roommates, and they'd done everything together. They'd traded in unfinished stories and reels of hope, most never making it past Bellamy's cutting table. Late nights with beers and schemes, sketching out the lives they'd lead once Hollywood took notice. They were a team.

But he hadn't been there the night Edmond decided. That had something to do with a moon-drenched evening on Olvera Street, if he recalled the conversation right. Edmond returned the next day rambling about lanterns and mariachis and how Rosalind—God help them—had worn just the right dress or laughed just the right way. The kind of laugh, the kind of night that made men want to buy houses. Settle down.

Writers.

Finch hadn't said much in response. He listened. But his wheels turned. He couldn't let a girl, no matter how special, shift the course they were on. Not now. They had plans, all three of them.

They were all part of Horace V. Bellamy's hand-picked film salon. Only the best and brightest were invited, and the whole affair unfolded on his own studio lot, the very backlot that had birthed pictures they all knew by heart. To most who sought his mentorship, Bellamy was the cinema itself. His stamp of approval could alter a destiny overnight.

Finch, Edmond, and Rosalind were among the lucky few, plucked from a crowd thinned without mercy. Some of the hopefuls were shipped back to dusty farms in Iowa or Kansas. Others boarded trains bound for backwater theaters in mining towns, or were sent across the Atlantic to Paris, Vienna, or London, told to seek fortunes where Bellamy's approval carried little weight. A number were dismissed with instructions to return to chorus lines, soda fountains, or sewing rooms in their hometowns, their film reels or scripts handed back like condolence notes.

No. The three of them were there for one reason only.

A proposal, a *marriage*, would derail everything and throw off the fragile balance the three of them had built. Besides, they were too young to think of such prospects. No, someone in Edmond's starry-eyed state wouldn't listen to reason. Finch would have to help in another way.

He remembered how Edmond dragged him through the jewelry markets. Finch had tried his best to seem supportive. So, there they stood, side by side in dungarees and caps, weighing carats, listening to sales pitches about clarity and debates over white or yellow gold. Finch added little but said the right things. He even held the ring up to the light, pretending to understand why that might be needed.

All the while, he couldn't help himself. He spent that night in a fever of thought, pacing the same mental hallway over and over. Edmond's plans would bring it all crashing down.

But there might be ways to stop it.

Young Finch, a bony youth with a straggling dark brown tangle atop his head, burst into the library. His face was pale, but his cheeks flushed. His eyes danced with a secret. He held a stack of papers in his hand and waved them as he approached Edmond and Rosalind.

"You'll never believe it. Not in a million years," young Finch said.

"Hey, come on now," Edmond said. "You're interrupting something important here."

"Yeah, give the love birds a moment alone, will ya?" Rosalind asked.

"Oh, hey, Crispy. I didn't see you there," Finch replied.

"Didn't see her there?" Edmond asked. He laughed. "How could you miss her?"

"Hey, watch it, boys! These curves have taken out better men than you...." Rosalind said.

"I doubt whether you'll look back and remember this as a ruined moment. I am about to deliver to you the greatest news of your life," Finch said. He huffed, breath catching like he'd just sprinted across the whole of Los Angeles.

"What are you going on about?" Rosalind asked.

Finch's eyes glowed with triumph. "Edmond, pack your bags. We're making that picture."

"Shut up, Bramwell. This is an awful prank to pull. One of your worst," Edmond said.

"Look," Finch said. He placed a stack of contracts in front of Edmond.

The young man raked his wild locks with stout fingers and inspected the documents.

"Bellamy? Bellamy signed off on a picture...? Your picture? But how?" Edmond asked. His expression flattened, as if the weight of possibility had landed square on it.

"You two will never believe it. Well, as you know, our final assignments have been due to him. And, well, I submitted your script to him," Finch said. "You can thank me now."

"Wait. You did what? You used *my* script and pretended you wrote it?"

Finch took Edmond's face in his hands. "Focus," he said. "Big picture. We're in. Bellamy loved it—all of it—and I cleared up any misconceptions. I told him who really wrote it."

He dropped his hands and paced while he spoke. "I showed Bellamy some scene sketches. Just rough ones I'd scribbled in the margins of my ledger. But the way you wrote, brother, I could see it all, every shot, every frame. And damn if Bellamy didn't sit up and say, '*You've got something here.*'"

Finch turned, grinning. "He wants me to direct. You supervise the script. We're fully funded. We're in."

Edmond gave a sideways glance to Rosalind. She shrugged.

"Jesus. I wasn't even finished writing *Moonlight Over Morocco*. I tossed it in the trash. It was just a practice script," Edmond said.

"And I thought it was brilliant, so I finished it myself. It was a comedy, right? Well, it is now. Do you realize what a break this is? No director, no *writer* in this town, let alone a kid in that film salon, gets Bellamy to sign off like this. You should have seen me schmooze the guy, and of course, we're practically making nothing for it."

He was panting, his face blotchy, and his voice sprinted toward the promise, the dream, before any of it might clear away.

"How exactly do I figure into this triumph? Seems like you've *managed* everything...." Edmond said.

"Aw, come on. You're getting all worked up over nothing," Finch replied. "I added only five pages, and I tried to make it all sound like you—bad poetry and all. Now listen. Bellamy's got us out in the Mojave with a crew of sixteen next Monday. Expects it to be finished in a month. Of course, there's post-production, editing, and they're letting us film in *Prismatone*. Bellamy said it was some kind of natural-color picture process. Did you hear that? Color. Of course, that takes time and assembly. So, we're looking at a November-December release." He clutched Edmond's shirt. "He's already cast the leads. Get this: Mabel LaRue and Douglas Montegue."

"November or December? That's going to be a year from now," Edmond said. He glanced at Rosalind. She had her hands cupped around her mouth, and her eyes looked like an unspoken pain was gathering behind them. "Can I talk to you for a minute?" He gestured to Finch to join him near the stacks.

Finch stepped aside with his friend. He had a grin, unguarded, boyish, as if it had nowhere else to go.

"Just what are you doing here? You came with me to Drucker's Diamond Jewelry last month. You knew I was going to propose. If you knew all along that you'd submitted the script to Bellamy, why did you let me get this far? Now I have to choose?" Edmond asked. He spoke in a harsh whisper. He eyed Rosalind, who sipped her coffee and tried to look like she wasn't listening or affected. But she crossed her legs, and one foot, free from the terrazzo floor, shook like a nervous cat's tail.

"Look, I gave Bellamy the script back in October. How was I supposed to know he'd bite? But isn't that why the three of us came to be a part of all this? So, what are you doing? You're going to get sidetracked by some *girl*? Are you nuts? You can propose to her or to any woman you want, any time you'd like once we make it big," Finch replied. "So, are you in or out?"

"Jesus, Bramwell. This is a goddamned awkward situation," Edmond said.

"Good," Finch replied. "Then, by your answer, I'm assuming you're choosing wisely. Besides, Rosalind isn't going anywhere. She's smart... just like you. You think she *wouldn't* take this opportunity if it came *her* way? Don't be a sap."

The elder Finch and the charred child watched from across the table.

"I... I can't imagine saying such things. I couldn't have," the older Finch said. "I would never ask him to choose like that. These were his decisions. His. I never forced anything."

The child pointed at Rosalind. It made a noise, but its throat was nothing but soot, so it only wheezed with a breathy squeak.

"Why can't they hear me? Why can't they...? I never said those things. These are lies! Who are you? Why don't you speak?"

The child's eyes oozed some black liquid that made a slow, inky path down his craggy cheek, but he kept pointing to the scene.

Edmond and young Finch returned to the table.

Rosalind sat up straight and fixed her expression. She refused to show what she felt about whatever the two of them had said. Edmond kept his gaze low. His smile flattened, then fell. She caught the shift, the pause, the silence that opened wide around the moment that the two of them had expected, the moment Finch knew they had discussed some time ago.

Her eyes filled, but she blinked them clear and set her jaw before either of the boys could see.

"That's..." Her voice hitched, and she cleared her throat. "That's incredible news, Bramwell. It is. A Christmas miracle."

"But darling, I can't go through with it... I can't make a picture like that. Not now," Edmond said. He took her hands in his. "I want you..."

"Edmond, listen to me. Yes, you *can* go through with it. And you will. If you don't choose this, you'll only end up hating me... at some point, yes. You'd grow to hate me," she said. "Bramwell is right. You can't let anything get in your way. Not now. You've worked too hard...."

She clamped her lips, and Finch watched as her eyes reddened and spilled over, but this time she didn't hide it.

"Don't, Rosalind," Edmond said. He brushed his thumb across her hand.

She looked at Finch, her expression unreadable. There were too many feelings fighting for room.

Then she slipped her hand from Edmond's, stood, and walked out the double doors. The only sound that followed was her heels squeaking on the floor. Finch thought how much they sounded like Sister Castor Oil's shoes. The same sound. The same squeak.

The elder Finch watched his younger self falter. His faint smile, the flicker of satisfaction, was already dimming before anyone could see it.

Elder Finch turned to the child. "No. No, that's not what I meant. It's a trick. Twisted. A distortion."

The boy pointed again. A distant projector whirred, then the scene changed.

SEVEN

THE FOREST AIR HAD teeth. It bit with dampness he hadn't felt since childhood. His feet went numb, planted in mud soaked through by icy rain.

The elder Finch watched a youthful likeness of himself traipsing through the fallen brown and orange leaves, stick in his hand, swiping at tree trunks as he passed them by. He wore his overalls with the pant legs tucked into brown rubber boots. The weather could change. The sky held its breath. More rain might follow. Maybe snow.

An older man with a goatee honed to a devilish tip marched behind holding a rifle. He was tall and slender but well set up. The boy would be like that one day. The man adjusted his hunting cap to warm his balding head. From his heavy jacket, he withdrew a silver flask. He unscrewed the top and took a long pull.

The boy turned. "Was mother crying again this morning?"

The man paused, flask still at his lips. His hand sank, the flask glinting in the gray light as he capped it tight.

"Crying's just noise, Bramwell. It doesn't mean anything unless you let it. That's a lesson some men learn too late."

He didn't look at the boy. Instead, he stared off at the crowding trees. The trunks and branches stood like old bones.

"Love makes men stupid. And stupid men deserve what they get."

The elder Finch swiveled his head, and he scanned the hillside. There, not far behind him, the small, scorched child in his charred little suit pointed to Finch's father.

"How are we here? In this place?" he asked.

But the child remained unspeaking, grinning with those perpetually charred teeth stretched into a ghastly smile across the hole where his lips had burned away. Finch could not stomach seeing him any longer, so he turned his attention back to the scene.

"That was my..." he said. He didn't want to say it. He felt a wave of nausea that he needed to suppress. "That man there... He was.... He was very proud of me." He felt himself deflate on those lies.

He eyed his younger self and observed him as he poked at an overturned wooden box, and he heard scrambling and scratching come from inside it. The younger Finch backed away and looked skeptical.

"Is it to be this way every time, Bramwell? Have you not a single ounce of manhood coursing through those milk-fed veins? Lift the damn box. Or are your lace cuffs in the way?"

"He had a temper. Yes. And so?" the elder Finch said. "But he saw something in me that needed help. Needed to be corrected. But on the whole, he understood me and provided what I could not find for myself."

The dead child standing at a distance, so somber, so grim, pointed onward at the scene.

Finch's father wiped brown drips of rye from his lips with his checkered sleeve.

"Do it," he said. It was more growl than words.

Young Finch approached and slid his fingers beneath the edge of the box. He lifted it, and beneath shivered a rabbit. The little gray thing looked up at young Finch and tried to dart away, but a wire loop snare his father had added to the trap caught its back foot. The animal squealed and struggled against the line.

"You didn't need to add that, father. I could have caught him with my hands," young Finch said.

"*I could have caught him with my hands.*" His father mocked the boy's voice, which had not yet matured and deepened. "We've been through this. Belt and suspenders, boy. Box trap and snare. Now go ahead."

He handed Bramwell the rifle.

"But father, can't I just pull the stake from the ground, pick him up, and carry him home?" Finch asked.

"Are you planning to put him in the oven like that, huh?" his father said. "Use your head. *Christ, you are the stupidest child.*"

The elder Finch heard those words, and they chewed through his heart. How often had he felt the bite of those words across his life?

Young Finch held the rifle, which was nearing the length of his body. He tried to balance it and point it toward the small creature. But as he aimed, his hand shook. He paused and took a deep breath. He leveled the shotgun and exhaled, but he did nothing more.

"I was too soft. Yes, he was right to tell me to do so. Yes, this was correct," the elder Finch said.

The burnt boy watched, and one of his smoking arms dropped to the ground. Elder Finch's insides recoiled. Not at the detached limb, but because he recognized the source of a sickness deep within, old and gangrenous, that had started in his soul.

The little dead boy seemed unaffected by his loss. He pointed with his other hand.

"Always trembling like a kicked pup. Can't even pull a simple trigger," his father said.

The young Finch reasserted himself. He looked like his limbs became steel girders. He hoisted the shotgun, and then he held his breath. His eyes widened, and sweat started on his forehead.

"Give me that, for Christ's sake," his father said. He yanked the rifle away from his son, who looked as though he'd had his hopes yanked along with it.

Finch's father scanned the hillside and looked like he might blow at any minute. Even the trees seemed to brace. Yes, Finch, young and old, knew the signs. The simmer had started, and it would erupt into a full explosion with the right source of ignition.

"Where the hell is he? Where's your friend?" he asked.

"He's not my friend. And I thought he was following us," young Finch said. "The last time I saw him, he was on the other side of the hill, looking at woolly caterpillars."

His father let out a sharp breath. "Oh, for the love of... caterpillars? Hopeless." He turned to his son, his fingers whitening around the rifle. "I better never catch you doing that."

He shouted. "Nathaniel!" His voice rolled like thunder through the valley, scattering birds to the sky.

He turned to his son. "If your mother hadn't insisted he come with us, I wouldn't be howling like a baboon. We'd be done clearing these traps by now."

"Mother said it was the Christian thing to do. He doesn't have a father now," young Finch said.

"Am I supposed to cry over it? His old man dies, and now we're meant to go trap-clearing like it'll fix him? People die. That's the only sure thing there is. If the boy didn't know that, he does now. And thanks to your mother, I'm saddled with the both of you."

Nathaniel never called back. Young Finch didn't move. He watched his father's hands, half expecting to see the rifle shift into gear. The boy swallowed, forcing back whatever threatened to rise in his throat.

His father scowled, and his pointed goatee bristled. "Well, don't just stand there, Bramwell. If you won't do what needs doing, then run along after your little friend and stop wasting my time."

The elder Finch stood from afar and watched the scene unfold. He remembered. He'd only been ten when his mother insisted they take Nathaniel along to help clear the small game traps.

Nathaniel's father had passed from pneumonia just weeks earlier. Once a respected city lawyer, he'd been disbarred in scandal and left with nothing but debts and shame. After losing his city flat, he moved his family to Ashwood Hollow, a place as cold and cheap as its reputation, far beneath the standards of Harrington Vale.

Finch knew Nathaniel from school in Stuyvesant Falls, where the children of Ashwood Hollow and the Vale were funneled into the same schoolhouse. But they never shared the same world. Not really.

None of Nathaniel's family was prepared for the harsh winters, and they paid the price. Bramwell didn't fully understand the rumors he'd overheard that Nathaniel's father once defended hopeless causes for little pay. But his own father spoke of the man as if he'd committed a crime.

"If he'd used his talents to win cases that paid instead of rescuing strays," he once told Bramwell, "he wouldn't be in a financial hole. Defend the poor long enough, and you become one of them."

The elder Finch watched the scene and felt his stomach tied into an impossible knot. He lost his breath. Or maybe his father took it from him long ago. He needed a moment to steady himself again.

He tried not to think of his father since his last day... when he watched them lower his sorry casket into the ground. Stray buckshot found his chest while hunting. An accident, they all said. Young Master Finch, all of sixteen years old, was at home the day it happened. Yes, he was at home with his mother.

The occurrence coincided with one of his mother's spells. She'd been prone to them after so many years of his father's cruelties, big and small. But after his father's death, she didn't just withdraw. She seeped inward, like rain dribbling away through long-rotted floorboards.

She lost awareness of the world around her and muttered to persons unknown and unseen. Over time, she took to her bed and lay there from sunrise to nightfall, day after day, for weeks.

The doctors couldn't explain what had undone her. Grief was common enough. But rarely did it bring a woman so low. Whatever her reasons, she kept them locked away.

But Finch knew. He'd tasted his father's cruel hand. After that last day at Harrington Vale Cemetery, she lost her ability to speak with each passing day. It was a slow retreat. And then she could not eat. Or sleep. And when her lips uttered words, they were disconnected and divorced from reality.

Bramwell would hear her pacing the plank floors long into the night. And sobbing. She'd weep in soft bouts, sometimes allowing a prolonged wail to escape her lips and float through the house like a hungry ghost. Bramwell covered his head with a pillow on nights like that and tried not to think of a heart mired in such grief.

One physician said she was melancholic and offered his tinted bottles of tiny round pills and powders she might mix into grain alcohol. None of them applied. They affected her as if she'd taken plain water. In time, the doctors called for men in long frock coats with their shackles to come to the Finch residence and remove her to their waiting black carriage with cage-windows.

Bramwell never saw her again, save for one Christmas, years later, at the *Harrowgate Asylum for the Utterly Insane.* She didn't know Bramwell or recognize him. She wore an ill-fitting, tattered wool gown, the same color as his father's grave, only filthier. And upon her withered breast lay her spittle and her falling white hair, tangled, matted, and shedding like threads from an old rag.

He held her hand and turned the key to a snow globe with Father Christmas inside. It played *Silent Night* to her, tinkling like a child's lullaby. She wept in silence. Not in pain, but in quiet ruin. Her tears seemed meant to clear away the wreckage of a life ill spent. She gazed into the distance, seeing some distant glory that defied the confines of her small, shabby cell.

He never returned after that Christmas. He didn't know whether she still lived and wasn't sure he wanted to.

The elder Finch watched as the younger version of himself stiffened his arms to his sides at his father's brusque command.

"Well, go, damn you. I swear, it's like splitting logs with two dandies. Run!" his father said. He pointed his rifle to the sky and pinched the trigger, sending a round from the chamber upward with a sound that boomed and reverberated through the land. The unexpected moment knocked young Finch into the mud. But he scrambled up and sped away, slipping through the wetted leaves and fallen twigs.

The elder Finch followed himself.

"Come back," the elder called. "He was only trying to make a point. Don't let him do this to you. Say something...."

Finch stopped at the burnt child who stood before him now in what was once an empty forest. He heard those last words, and they carried crushing weight with them. He felt his lips pinch and his vision blur with what felt like tears. But he wouldn't let some vision, some hallucination or dream impact him like that. So, he stuffed it all down again.

The elder Finch edged around the blackened child and followed his younger self through the foliage and over logs.

"Don't go there! Do you hear me?" Finch said.

He saw his younger self run faster, darting glances over his shoulder as though he knew the unseen specter of his older self hunted him. As though he never wanted to become whatever his father had created in the future.

The boy pressed on, upward and back down the other side of the hill, stumbling on a stone hidden beneath a sopping, slippery leaf pile, and he tumbled forward. Down, down he slid through the hill's rotting clutter, until at last he lay panting. Young Finch got to his knees and watched through eyes wide with terror for which he lacked words. But he knew his father might not be far behind. And men like him didn't stop with a simple shout or a warning shot.

He waited low to the ground. But when the man did not step over the ridge as expected, he ventured onward.

"Nathaniel," young Finch called. "Nathaniel, come out."

The elder Finch stood on the hillside listening to himself as a boy, so desperate, so nearing the point of brokenness. He'd heard that same voice from his mother. But it was Nathaniel who now faced danger. No matter what he thought of the boy, he didn't want to take responsibility for the outcome of his father's drunken wrath.

Young Finch called Nathaniel's name again, almost a cry, while he trod through an ankle-deep marsh thick with reeds. There, he found Nathaniel standing like a pale statue erected in a strange child wax museum.

The elder Finch followed, though he knew this scene. And he felt a darkness coming upon him—one he had always managed to outrun. At least until now.

"Nathaniel! We've been looking for you for..."

Young Finch stopped when Nathaniel turned toward him. His white sailor's knickers, the ones with brass buttons down either side of his pelvis, had bright yellow stains that ran down the inner thigh of one leg. He held a hefty branch in one hand. Young Finch noted dark, wet splotches upon it that had smeared onto his balled fist. Red. Dark red.

"I couldn't stop myself. I didn't mean to. I just couldn't stop," Nathaniel said.

His eyes were wide and staring, but at nothing in particular.

"What did you do?" young Finch asked.

Nathaniel repeated himself and sounded more robotic than human. "I just... couldn't... stop."

He finished the last word as though he'd drifted off to sleep, though his eyes looked as though he'd discovered some terrible secret.

Young Finch saw the box trap lowered, as though it served its purpose and caught small game. But from the bottom of the box, trailing into the pond, was a bloody seepage, dark and dank, thick as though pounded from inner organs.

Before Finch had a moment to clear it, and to hide Nathaniel, his father came from behind. He lifted the box up with his hunting shoe and saw what Nathaniel had done with that club.

"There. You see, Bramwell? Even a boy like Nathaniel understands what must be done. Though you didn't leave much for us to eat. I'm proud of you, boy. You did a man's job today."

His father turned to young Finch and spoke to him as though he was an incidental body, and an annoying one at that.

"Clean this mess up, Bramwell. Ah, Nathaniel, my boy. You've made an old man proud. Now let's go get you washed up."

Finch's father placed an arm around the child with the delicate shoulders, who looked as if he'd been bewitched, staring straight ahead, lips moving in the same broken refrain. He moved with the older man, dazed, like a sleepwalker.

Young Finch remained, staring at the mess Nathaniel had left behind.

The elder Finch watched as his father guided Nathaniel.

"He was my father," the elder Finch said. "*My* father."

The charcoal child with his smoking skin pointed off to the side.

The scene blurred, and Finch heard the mechanical clicking of the projector somewhere in the hazy distance, but nowhere to be seen.

They stood inside the living room of a well-appointed lodge. Bramwell's father had it constructed to a standard he believed was rustic, though it was grand and sprawling across the Catskill Mountain acreage. Logs stacked and interlocked, but inset glittering windows overlooked panoramic views.

"Bramwell?"

Young Finch turned from the fireplace, where he'd just finished straightening the shotgun above the mantel.

"Bramwell, are you downstairs?"

His mother's voice floated down from the floor above, warm, expectant, and just a touch too bright to be believed.

The deer heads on either side of the mantel watched him with their dead black eyes glimmering in the firelight.

His mother drifted down the steps in her gown with lace up the throat. One hand trailed the banister, as though she weren't entirely sure the floor would be there when she reached it. She smiled as though her memories were trying to take their shape when she spotted him in front of the cheery fire, warming his hands.

"Well, that's a pretty picture. How many Christmases has it been with the three of us here? How is it you've become a young man without me noticing? Oh, we'll have a marvelous Christmas, won't we, Bramwell? Just the three of us. And we'll be happy. We *will* be happy, won't we? Tell me we will."

She seemed to look through him and to speak to the Elder Finch, who stood close to the charred child.

His younger self nodded to her, but he watched her with care. She was rambling again, trying to will joy into existence. Another nervous spell, he realized. It might last for days. It might go on longer now. She was slipping.

He looked back toward the mantel, avoiding her eyes. The fire crackled, and an uneasy silence filled the space between her words and her upspoken expectations. The room felt too warm, the silence too loud, and the walls seemed too near.

"Did you hear that just now?" she asked. She darted to a window, pressed her hands against the glass. "Was that a shot? Did you hear it? Of course you did. That must be your father. He's out there. He's always out there."

The elder Finch remembered that smile. It was always faint and uncertain, as if worn for everyone else's sake.

She stayed there, palms pressed to the pane. Her breath left little clouds against the glass. She rested her cheek against the frozen pane.

"Even in the snow," she said. "He knows his way around the woods. You know that, don't you?"

Bramwell nodded and tucked his lips. He stole another glance at the deer heads that made him feel uncomfortable, their slitted eyes glistening in the firelight, too wide, too unfeeling.

Always watching, knowing.

"Well, never you mind. *He's a great hunter*. He knows his way around the woods, doesn't he?" she asked.

She let out a laugh, but the sound was as fragile as a newly formed crust of ice. Finch watched her with care. Her eyes didn't settle on anything. Tears gathered, reflecting firelight like the deer on the wall. She turned away from the window and began fussing with the garland of holly that decorated the mantel beneath the rifle. She touched the gun, and then her lips.

Her tone was bright again, and her smile quivered.

"Did he ever tell you about his long voyage to Africa? His safari there? Oh, he was a grand hunter. That lion's pelt by the fireplace came back with him. That's your father... he's a hunter... through and through," she said.

Her voice faltered. She scurried back to him, clutching his head in both hands.

"And so are you. His son. His brave son."

She stiffened, her smile collapsed. Her voice dropped to a whisper. "Did you hear that, Bramwell? Was that... was that a shot? You heard it. I know you did. You heard it, too."

Both young and old Finch watched her, but had no words.

She whispered, "Your father's a great hunter. And you... you take after him, don't you?"

She cradled young Finch, tightening her grip, squeezing him with a strength he never knew she had.

She whispered in his ear. "We'll be happy, won't we, Bramwell? We'll have the happiest of Christmases, won't we?"

The deer heads on the wall watched him, their glassy eyes, wide-set and unblinking.

The charnel child standing in the corner pointed off yet again.

EIGHT

THE ELDER FINCH SQUINTED as the Regent Motorworks limousine pulled to the curb. The images were off. Clicking. Shuddering. And then they stilled. He remembered the flashbulbs, but not the smell of burning hair.

Boomf. Boomf-boomf. The magnesium ignited the night like a cannonade. He held a hand up to shield his eyes. The younger Finch did not.

The flash pans and their blinding light continued while Finch and Malvern, looking like sleek seals in silk-lapelled tuxedos, marched together up the steps to the *China Pacific Theater*. Their hair was slicked back, and their smiles were those of men who knew they were launching into the stratosphere.

The elder Finch winced at the bursts of light, but the younger one basked in them. They emerged from that limousine like kings, dressed in their evening black and borrowed bravado. He felt immortal under that unrelenting glare. And the elder Finch remembered it well. But he didn't feel the warm glow of nostalgia. Instead, he remembered it all with a slow, rancid pull in his gut.

He had forgotten how young they all were. How untouchable they believed they were.

The theater loomed like an ancient emperor's palace transplanted to Hollywood Boulevard, its façade a riot of gilded dragons, golden columns, and an ornate jade-green roof that curled like a pagoda against the starry sky. Below the roofline hung a white banner like drapes across a wire line. *Premiering Tonight: Dusk Over Savannah.*

Movie goers cheered the pair, who waved to them as they ascended the short steps and entered the ornate lobby.

The incinerated child stood by the door and pointed so the elder Finch would follow them inside.

The ceiling, vaulted and painted with elaborate depictions of gold-leaf-trimmed pagodas and dragons, soared above. Once the soaring heavy doors closed behind them, the cavernous entry held the hushed stillness of the air just before a thunderclap.

"Did you see that crowd, Bramwell?" Edmond asked.

Finch smiled and withdrew cigars from his vest pocket. He lit them up and puffed Edmond's to life before handing it to him.

"I saw Horace V. Bellamy out there," Finch said. He puffed a ring of smoke above Edmond's head. "He must be green with envy by now."

"Mmm. Carrington Black, too," Edmond added.

"Black? That old phony? I thought he was still recovering from *When the Camellias Fade*," Finch said.

"*Vault & Reel* says he's running *Majestic Pictures* now."

"Majestic? Then that explains their last three disasters."

The two men laughed and threw their arms around each other's shoulders.

"Now let's see if your bet on this Lola Fontaine pays off," Finch said. He looked like he tasted the bitterness in every word.

"Relax, Bramwell," Edmond said. "She's gorgeous and plays to the camera like a kitten on a lamb's wool rug."

"I can't get it out of my mind that I've seen her somewhere before," Finch said. "Where did you say you found her?"

"Nowhere you'd ever go. All you need to know is she met our criteria. She had the curves that kept the cameramen awake, and she worked for cheap," Edmond said. He grinned like he was clever.

"Emphasis on the word cheap," Finch said. He puffed smoke from the side of his mouth. "Still, a pair of standouts and no union card is always a solid business plan," Finch said.

"Look, all that matters tonight is our first picture as CineFilm. Jesus, Bramwell, our first picture without another studio backing us, and we're at the China Pacific," Edmond said. "Do you know how many production outfits there are now in Hollywood? Christ, half of them started just after us, and most of them would kill to land a premiere here. Most of them are lucky to start off at the *Pharoah* or the *Footlight*."

From the balcony staircase descended Rosalind in a shimmering white gown, jeweled and fitted to every curve. An enormous fluff of white fox formed a cloud collar around her pale ballerina's neck.

The elder Finch inhaled sharp and quick. Rosalind. He'd forgotten how radiant she was that night. She wasn't the red-carpet type, not with her tortoise-shell and sensible oxfords. But for this, she'd shed the glasses and gave any screen goddess a run for her money.

Edmond nodded to her then returned his attention to the younger Finch.

"You're right. And I'll admit Lola's got allure," younger Finch said. "It might be the kind that comes with aliases... But you're right. Let's focus on tonight and the success we owe to you. To your vision. To your casting...."

"Not to mention my script," Edmond said.

"So, in honor of tonight, I'll reserve judgement of Miss Fontaine until we see what the *Times-Mirror* has to say about her," Finch said.

A man in a tight suit slipped through the side door. "Gentlemen. There's a minor issue with the *OrchestraTone* sound system."

"Then fix it," Finch said. He kept his back to Rosalind.

She sighed. "Well, here's a howdy-do. And to think, I nearly wore something attention-grabbing."

"Hello darling. Just a moment," Edmond said.

Rosalind whispered in Finch's ear. "I'll just assume you're struck speechless."

"Honestly, Edmond, I'll have to rely on your expert opinion here. Do women always need an audience?" Finch asked.

"Did I miss the part where we're all pretending I'm invisible?" she asked.

Edmond took Rosalind's hands and kissed them.

"Darling, you heard the man. There're technical problems. Can you wait?" he asked.

Finch addressed the manager. "You were saying? The sound issue?"

Rosalind tilted her head and looked struck.

"No, you're right, Bramwell. Why notice someone two feet away when there's a sound system in peril? Wait until the OrchestraTone finds out how much you need it to adore you...."

"Now Rosalind...." Edmond said.

Finch rolled his cigar between his fingers.

"At least a film knows when to stay silent."

He had said that, hadn't he? Even now, the words rang with cruelty. The elder Finch winced at the sound of his own voice. It still landed like a lash. From this vantage, he saw everything more clearly. He had thought himself so clever. But now he watched Rosalind shrink beneath his remark, watched the way his words poisoned the air around her.

The younger Finch turned to the stage manager.

"Can I meet with the technician? Good. Let's see what we can do."

All three men turned to leave, but Rosalind pulled Edmond back by his arm.

"Listen, Edmond. We really need to talk," she said.

"Can it wait? There's a crowd outside," Edmond said.

"There's always something, isn't there?"

"What?"

"Finch. You. This business. I wasn't going to say anything tonight. But from the looks of things, this will never end, will it? This business. *Him*. You're consumed... both of you."

"Rosalind. Come on. You're being... well, you're being absurd. You're smart enough to know how competitive this business can be. You know what this film means for us. And at one point, *you* wanted it, too."

"I did," she said. "Once. But I don't know anymore. Now that I see what it's done to you... to me... Finch made sure CineFilm would never really include me."

"What do you mean? We're just getting started," Edmond said. "The studio system may not recognize your talents, not this second. But it will. Once we've opened the door, we'll pull you through...."

"Yes. I know what the studios want. And it's not women. At least not for the heavy lifting. They'll take us for makeup and sequins, sure. It's not enough, Edmond. *We're* not enough."

"*We*? What are you saying?" he asked.

She lowered her voice, steady as a prayer. Her hand rose to his cheek, trembling.

"We once talked about marriage. A life together. But every time I reached for you... he was already there. Every meeting. Every choice. He got to you first. And I waited. And waited. But you stopped looking for me. Can you really say otherwise?"

Edmond pulled away and raked a hand through his hair.

"That's not fair," he said.

"No. But it's true. And it's not all Finch's fault. You chose him. Or you let him choose for you."

"Look. There are reporters outside. Everything's riding on tonight. You can't expect me to just walk away from my future," he said.

"No. I don't. And you're right. This is *your* future, Edmond. I just don't see a place in it for me."

She motioned toward the high ceilings and the glittering dragons looming overhead.

"You'll never give this up. Or him. Not if he takes you where you want to go. And I've never been any good at waiting in the wings."

She pressed the ring he'd given her into his palm.

The elder Finch watched Edmond's fingers close around it, saw Rosalind's linger a moment too long, as if her hand alone carried hope.

She looked into Edmond's eyes but saw nothing but distraction.

"Rosalind. What are you doing?" he asked.

Her words were soft, measured. "You may have the spotlight now," she said, "but at least I'm not standing in the dark anymore."

She pulled the fur collar tight around her neck, as though she felt a chill, as though she realized how cold the world was now. She turned to the tall doors, and the ushers on either side opened them. She vanished into the waiting camera flashes.

Malvern turned away. He never saw her leave. But the elder Finch did. He saw everything, too late. He wished he could call her back. But he couldn't. Not now.

The brooding boy with coal-black hands pointed again. The sound of the projection room clicked and sputtered in the atmosphere.

In a split second, Finch was in a doctor's consultation room. Diplomas and framed certificates lined the paneled walls.

Rosalind sat across from him, biting her lip.

A man in a white lab coat with a reflective mirror strapped to his forehead held a clipboard and scanned it. "You can always go to Saint Cyprian's for a therapeutic procedure. They'll conduct it, if a doctor provides some... justification."

She nodded in silence and cupped her hands around her abdomen. She was showing now. It was small, but obvious. Soon others would notice.

"There's always Mexico," he added. "Does your husband know?"

She clutched her purse like it might fly away.

"Thank you, doctor. I appreciate you taking the time..."

The elder Finch watched, and the fire-marked boy pointed away from the scene.

"I didn't know why she'd disappeared," Finch said. The words came smooth and quick, worn down by use. "I knew she was angry with me. She had a child. But I never asked who the father was. I never wanted to know."

The disfigured child shook its head, and Finch heard the skin crackle. It insisted Finch look elsewhere now with his pointing arm until his second limb dropped free. It hit the floor with a sickening squish. The fingers twitched. The shoulder from where it had torn smoked like old wood doused in fire. But the finger remained pointing out to the distance.

NINE

SOMEWHERE IN THE DARK, the sounds of the projector kept churning, churning, like a furnace engine grinding out some unknown factory quota.

Beyond it, white stretched to an endless horizon. There Finch saw a hillside blanketed in snow, its silence absolute.

The child, reduced to embers, stood with the blackened remnants of his tie at his neck. He stood out against the new-fallen snow, all charred flesh, and his clothing still smoldering. He watched Finch with his gelatinous eyes. Both of his arms were gone now, so he bowed his head in the direction he wanted Finch to see.

Neither of them spoke. The wind picked up, tugging at Finch's coat. Panic rose in his throat like bile, but he forced it back down, hard, where it belonged.

Indignation was his safer default. The heat of frustration had a grounding familiarity.

"Who are you?" he asked. His voice came out sharper than he expected. "I've asked before, and still, you remain mute like a gravestone. Say something, damn you."

He took a step forward, his breath clouding in the frozen air. He had no more shouts or anger left to shield him. He was only spitting words to keep the silence from taking him.

The child bowed his head.

A memory stirred beneath the ice. Dread settled inside him, and he could find no respite from it. He pulled his coat tighter, but warmth did not follow.

"What do you want from me?" His voice faltered. "You should be in a hospital or... or buried in a churchyard. Not...." He stopped. "Not standing there."

The child watched him with those ruined, weeping eyes. Still silent. Still burning.

Then he turned his face toward the hill behind them. The same hill Finch had once known as a child.

Boys rushed downward on their toboggans and shouted in excitement for the two girls below to clear away. The girls screamed, threw snowballs at them, and dodged aside to avoid being run over.

A boy, no higher than a man's waist, stood watching.

The broiled boy next to Finch bowed his head to the child standing alone.

"What is it you want me to see?" Finch asked. "It's only children playing in the snow."

Finch glanced and noticed the specter had moved. He stood armless and smoking beside the lonely child.

"I don't know what you're about, but you can't keep me here," he said.

Finch turned to leave, but the entire scene with tobogganers and screaming girls was again in front of him.

"How can this be?"

The corpse child stared at the boy standing alone.

Finch knew what it wanted. But he dared not see.

The toboggan came to a halt, and the three boys riding it whispered to one another.

The tallest of the three called to the boy all alone. "Nathaniel! Nathaniel Thorne! Come, take a ride."

Nathaniel backed up in his rubber boots and shook his head. There was a look in his eyes that Finch knew. Nathaniel turned his attention away and scoured the hillside for a place to hide. But there was nothing. Just the outhouse. And that had gone wrong before.

"Nathaniel, Nathaniel, soft and meek,
Walks with a wiggle and pink on his cheek!
Talks like a lady, dressed all neat,
Tiptoe, tiptoe, light on his feet!"

The boys sang their rhyme and laughed. Nathaniel attempted to run, but his rubbers slipped, and he toppled face first into the white powder.

The boys crunched through the drifts and surrounded him. All three lifted him and dragged Nathaniel, bloody nose and all, to the top of the hill. His head rolled back and forth on a loose neck, as though he were half stunned.

The girls linked arms and stood in the boys' path.

"Bramwell! Rufus! Jasper! You boys leave him alone," one said.

"You shut up, Margaret Lester. Or you'll be next," Jasper snapped.

He had one eye that always wandered in another direction. Some said it was glass. Others swore it was wood. One rumor claimed it had wood worms.

"Why are you ruining his Christmas Day?" Margaret asked.

Her friend lost her nerve. She seemed startled by Margaret's defiance, stepped back, and stared down at the snow.

"Boys, I think we've heard enough from Miss Margaret Le*Snitch*," young Finch said. "Who cares what day it is? No one cares about Christmas, Margaret. You're just upset because it's not another school day when you can pucker your lips on Miss Eugenia's backside."

"You watch your language, Bramwell Finch! I'll tell your father," Margaret said.

Young Finch pushed Margaret in the center of her chest, sending her into the snow.

"Look, boys. A dirty snitch!" he said.

"I'm not a snitch," Margaret said.

"Then you two clear out," Finch said.

Margaret's friend helped to pick her back up, and she brushed the snow from her back.

The older Finch watched then turned his attention to the ruined little ghost.

"Won't you do something? You won't just stand there and let this happen, will you?"

The ashen cadaver nodded but said nothing.

The girls clung to one another, too afraid to move. Jasper and Rufus knew Bramwell had them under control, so they kept dragging the near-unconscious Nathaniel up the hill, which was higher and steeper than any of them would ever dare ride themselves.

Finch followed, pulling the toboggan behind him.

Nathaniel's rubbers dragged, and one slipped off, left limp and forgotten in the snow.

The boys laid him, stomach first, on the toboggan and laughed as he awakened and groaned. Young Finch approached from behind and gave the sled a final shove with his foot.

The three of them hooted as it flew down, like a hawk dropping from the sky.

The wind hit Nathaniel's face, cold and stinging. His eyes opened. He gasped and twisted, planting his arms where his feet should go. Then he screamed.

"Steer it, Nathaniel! Steer it!" Margaret said. "Hold the rope!"

Nathaniel's descent ended soon after it began. Thrashing for control, he veered into a bank of trees. The toboggan shattered on impact. His body pitched forward, striking a trunk with a sickening thud and a crack of bones. Snow from the branches above slipped loose and buried him. Then, silence.

The boys laughed while Margaret and her friend trudged through the mounds of fresh snow to dig Nathaniel out.

The boys mimicked his scream, flapping their hands like butterflies until they saw the girls standing over a crumpled body, limbs bent in wrong directions, pale face turned to the sky.

Margaret screamed.

The boys fell over one another in their hasty scramble to see the wreckage for themselves.

"You better not be exaggerating, Margaret. Someone better be dead," young Finch said. "If not, you two are taking a ride, too."

The boys shoved the girls aside, and they stopped laughing. They saw Nathaniel's eyes open, as though he could still see, still hear, but he did not stir.

"Oh, Jesus," Finch said. He reached down to pull Nathaniel's body up, but there was too much snow covering him still. "Well, don't just stand there," he said.

Jasper and Rufus got to their knees and dug away the surrounding snow with their mittens, but when they pulled Nathaniel out, he was limp and unresponsive.

Finch looked paler than usual.

Margaret dropped on all fours and placed an ear to Nathaniel's chest. "Nathaniel! Nathaniel, please," she cried.

But his head lolled backward, his neck gone slack.

"You beast, Bramwell. Look what you've done. You're in for it now."

Nathaniel's lips started looking pale. Then they turned blue.

"Shut up. Shut up!" Finch said. "If you say a word. One word...."
He approached her with his hand balled in a sturdy fist.

The other girl, Lucy, who accompanied Margaret, found her voice
and shouted, "Leave us alone! Leave him alone. I'll kill you all!"

She picked up a fallen branch and held it aloft. But after she made
her threat, she turned the color of the hillside, dropped the wood, and
shivered in silence.

"I know where you both live. I know where to find you. Say a word
to anyone... anyone, and you'll regret it," young Finch said.

"What are we going to do?" Jasper asked. Of all of them, Jasper was
the most likely to ask. He stood most of the time in the teacher's corner
wearing the dunce hat.

"We're taking him back to his house," Finch replied.

"Are you crazy? If anyone sees? They'll put us in orphanages or
asylums," Rufus said.

Finch observed the two girl's dresses.

He glared at Margaret and Lucy. "Look at you. You're covered in his
blood."

"What? What are you talking about?" Margaret asked.

Finch withdrew a pocketknife and sliced Nathaniel's hand. From it
came a thick red ooze that he collected in his palm.

Lucy screamed and tried to run.

"Don't let them leave," Finch said.

The two boys held Margaret and Lucy in place. Finch pulled
Nathaniel's blood-dripping hand closer to the girls. They recoiled with
screams. Finch held off smearing them.

"We'll drag him to his mother's barn and lay him in the hay," he
said. "Set the place on fire. It'll be an accident. And if anyone finds out
what happened otherwise, who do you think they'll blame? Not us.

We won't have blood on our clothes. But you? Margaret? Lucy? We'll say you pushed him. We'll say you tried to cover it all up, and that we saw you two take him to the barn."

The girls looked at one another and tried squirming away. But Rufus and Jasper were too big, too strong for them.

"And when I tell them you did it, they'll take you away. Maybe hang you both," he said.

"All right," Lucy said. "All right. I won't tell. Margaret... please Margaret, you need to swear it."

Margaret stood in her snow-drenched outfit, her eyes staring like she'd seen the devil step out of the dark and smile at her.

"I swear," Margaret said. She gritted her teeth, flared her nostrils, and glared at Finch, locking eyes with him, no longer afraid of anything he might do to her now.

"I thought so," Finch said. "Rufus, Jasper, take him."

It wasn't what they expected. None of them. But neither was Nathaniel crashing on the toboggan.

Finch ran back to them, as Lucy, Margaret, Jasper, and Rufus were all too afraid of this final step. It had been an accident up to now.

They huddled together just behind the tree line of pine and maple as young Finch tore up chunks of snow that flicked off the backs of his boots, with steam puffing from his open mouth. The barn was too far from their hidden ridge for them to make out much detail. They didn't want to see, anyway.

"Were there animals inside, Bramwell? There better not have been," Lucy said.

Finch nodded and put his hands on his knees while he huffed and tried to catch his breath.

"There was an old white goat. But it wouldn't leave. It reared up and tried to gore me when I got too close," Finch said.

"Did you untie it?" Margaret asked. Didn't you at least untie it?" Margaret asked.

"Shut up, both of you," Rufus said.

"Yes, I untied it," Finch said.

Licks of flame lit the late afternoon sky now, interrupting their argument.

"Come on, let's get out of here," Finch said. "And remember what I promised if you say anything..."

"Bramwell... oh, *Bramwell*, do you hear that?" Margaret asked.

"There's nothing. Come on, let's go," Jasper said.

"No, I hear him. *I hear him*," Margaret said.

She squirmed from Jasper's grip and scrambled up the snowy embankment. She laid on her stomach and cupped her hands on her face.

"I hear something too," Rufus said. "You don't hear it?"

"Hear what? Come on. Before anyone gets here," young Finch said.

Then Finch heard it, too. Screams. Soft. Like crying. They all scrambled up the snow slope and watched the barn, which was now a mass of orange flames, belching black smoke from the hayloft and from between roof planks.

"Let me out. Can't you hear me? No. No! Let me out!"

"Nathaniel! You can't let him die, Bramwell. Get him out!" Margaret said.

"But he was... you said he was.... He was cold. He wasn't breathing," Finch said.

"Help! Oh, God. Help me!" Nathaniel's small voice tore up the sky. That shut them all up.

The light had faded to purple, and the stars offered their small, wavering light. Finch was about to risk it all and cross the white-blanketed meadow when Nathaniel's mother came around the side of the barn. She carried an axe and a lamp. The barn door was too hot, and when she tried to open it, she fell backward, shoving her hands in the snow.

The whole time, Nathaniel's cries pierced the sky, the meadow, their souls. They watched as she stood again and chopped at the door. But she hadn't any strength in her hands after she'd burned them, and she fell backward, sobbing, pounding her fists into the slush.

"Bramwell! Go help," Lucy said.

"Go help!" the elder Finch yelled. He stood behind his younger image. "Go! Oh, my God, go!"

The children backed away... all except young Finch. He stayed anchored to the fateful scene.

Nathaniel's mother tried again. She'd torn fabric from her dress and wrapped her hands in it. Then she resumed chopping and chopping while fighting against her long, ruffled skirt and her high-necked blouse. The barn roared, hotter than ever.

There was a sound like thunder that echoed in the children's ears. It was the sound of the barn collapsing in on itself.

The elder Finch watched, and his chest buckled inward with the weight of his deed, as if no years had passed, as if time itself had collapsed. It was done, and there was no one else to blame. The noose of guilt cinched hard, and every breath felt wrenched from the air around him. The snow near the barn turned black and orange with soot and flame while he stood side by side with his younger self, doing nothing but bearing silent witness in horror.

The barn went silent. Nathaniel's voice was gone. His mother had no more tears. And the sky, at last, darkened.

She folded into the ash, rocking, her hands burned red, her voice torn. And it rose to the moon as something animal, ancient, and aching with a sorrow that escaped the capture of words.

From the smoldering of the ruins, Finch saw the goat emerge. The creature, once white with four horns, was now stained with smears of ash and a color deeper than coal matting its beard.

"He got out," young Finch whispered.

Then the goat reared up on its hind legs and watched, as though it knew both the elder and the younger Finch were there, hiding in the woods along with their shame.

The ice crept through his shoe soles like knives, and with it came a dread he thought he'd long buried.

"No..." he said. He whispered the rest. "Nathaniel was dead. He was already... dead."

The spirit child, destroyed by fire, looked at him with his oozing eyes and nodded toward the barn. Toward Nathaniel's mother, sobbing in the frost. Then at Finch.

The elder Finch buckled. The younger mirrored his movements.

They fell to their knees, faces in their hands. The cries came harsh and broken, ripped from their throats like confessions. Neither meant to crumble so. But the sorrow forced its way out. The grief had scraped up, raw and unfettered.

"I didn't mean to..." the elder Finch said. "I was... I was only a child. I didn't know. I didn't...."

He trailed off, because he *knew*. He knew enough.

The small smoldering spirit didn't move or speak. He didn't need to.

TEN

"I DIDN'T MEAN TO..." Finch said. He'd sunk to his knees, clutching at the scorched remnants of the boy's clothing.

He opened his eyes and saw himself. He was somewhere else, or at least his image was not where he knelt. A second version of himself stood at a distance, foggy and flickering, grainy.

The broiled Nathaniel no longer bore witness to Finch's memories. Now it was only Finch and himself.

He approached the ghostly self-image, reaching for it. It wasn't insubstantial; it was just elsewhere.

A translucent, unnatural barrier kept him from reaching his double. But there he was.

Clickety-click. Clickety-click. The projector on the far side of the strange veil chattered on, driven by some ghostly engine. It clicked along on the other side of this uncanny surface. He watched himself lie on the floor of the small preview room, making unearthly wails, which were not so much crying as unraveling. They were more human, more vulnerable than he'd ever allowed.

And yet, as he watched, he felt his own sadness rise. It was vast and cold, like the tide swelling in a moonless winter darkness. It filled his throat, and he sobbed in perfect time with the image across from him.

Something shifted inside him, quiet and seismic. As if his bones remembered what was awful before he did. He wasn't holding

Nathaniel's tattered remains. No. He was clutching the red velvet drapes that flanked the screening room screen.

Before he could stop it, he was there on the screening room floor, at one with the man he saw sobbing, choking on regrets that he supposed were long-abandoned in a forgotten wintry past. The fabric in his hands was heavy, still warm, as if it clung to Nathaniel's fire.

"I didn't mean to..." He said it without effort, without intention. And in saying it, the weight atop his chest loosened and allowed him breath. Old sorrow withdrew back into shadow.

He released the drapes and began collecting himself. His clothes, his hair, his dignity, each disheveled, wrecked, as though a hurricane had passed through, sparing nothing.

He didn't believe in carrying on like this. Not even after Edmond. Sentimentality, tear-stained cheeks, faltering speech were indulgences he'd never permitted in himself or anyone else. His father had called such displays "performance." They led to the strap.

What trembled inside him broke loose into laughter, though he could not tell why.

Then he realized, this was *Runaway Reckoning*. That's all. He was dreaming of that overwrought script Victor tried to salvage with directing alone. And what came out was overwritten and overstated. It was full of melodramatics that no one would believe.

And here he was. *Runaway*.

"Look at you," came a voice. It was as smooth as a drag on a cigarette. "You've finally reached the bottom of the cutting room floor, haven't you, Finchy?"

"Who...? Who is that?" Finch asked. He righted himself and wiped his face. She crossed the room; her glittering heels made no sound. Strange. Yet he'd seen that before. Yes, Saint Cyprian's. Sister Zagan walked the floor as though she hovered.

"Tragic, isn't it? After all those reels you've trimmed, and yours has the nerve to play uncut," Vivian said. The reel continued to click on behind her. Relentless. Harsh. As though it burned forward on Nathaniel's fire. He'd never noticed how the sound grated on him. It was always music before this. Cash in the drawer.

The projector threw its moving light across the room. When it hit her face, he recognized her. Vivian Delacroix. Same slinky gown from the Laurel Awards showing all her rubbery curves. The dress was too young, too low, and the hem too high for someone who'd played monarchs.

She held a martini and sipped from it.

"What are you doing here?" he asked.

"Oh, darling, pull yourself together. You'll never win a Laurel like this." She gave a lazy wave of her martini then skewered him with a stare rimmed in rouge and liner.

"Unless they've added a category for *Most Tragic Offscreen Breakdown*," she added.

"You can't be here. It's after hours. You... you need an appointment. We've closed auditions for *Whispers on the Stair*," he said. "You'll have to come back another... another time."

He heard himself. It didn't sound right. None of this did.

Vivian picked it up like a dropped microphone.

"Tomorrow's Christmas, Finchy. Looks like you skipped the frankincense and myrrh and jumped straight to the noose," she said.

He straightened and tried to look as though he belonged.

"Vivian. Good night. See yourself out. I'm... busy."

She sipped. Eyes glinting in the light.

"I can see that. Some reels don't age well, do they? *Scandalous*, really."

"Vivian. You're trying my patience. If you won't leave, I'll call security. And that would be most satisfactory, so don't tempt me."

He moved to the phones. But from the dark below the seats, she lifted Edmond's severed head by the hair.

"*Choo-Choo*! Malvern turned out to be an *absolute* train wreck," she said. "Though I suppose it's his fault for stepping off script. Another one for your rejection pile?"

He felt like she'd plunged him into ice cold water. His breath left his body and hovered somewhere nearby until he found it again. She advanced, holding the head. Edmond was milky-eyed, and his mouth hung open. Sinew still dangled from the neck like a ribbon from a tattered gift. Finch scrambled backward and shouted. His jaw quivered, his head felt fizzy, and he tipped to one side, but caught his balance.

"What in God's name are you holding there? I'll call the police… I'll—"

He staggered, tripped, and landed on a leather couch behind him. The room had shifted. Fireplace roaring. A Christmas tree blazing with lights. Wrapped boxes like red and green lies piled at its feet.

"I did tell him, but here we are," Horace Bellamy said.

His voice boomed, broad and oiled like a salesman's pitch. His beard was thick as black wool, and his eyebrows looked like commas that had escaped a script.

"Well, it's his loss," Vivian said. She lounged near Finch's head. He sat up and gazed at her.

"Looks like he's on quite the losing streak."

"I told you I was going to call the police, and I will, you moth-eaten cinematic has-been," Finch said.

But she didn't budge. She smiled and sipped her martini like nothing mattered more.

"I was told he'd been having a breakdown," another woman said. Her voice was a scratchy whisper. She wore a glittering black ensemble that had peaked ten years prior. She took a long drag from her cigarette holder and blew the smoke upward.

"A long, slow breakdown."

"Finch? Oh, darling, that's old news," Vivian said. "He's been cracking like the plaster at Monarch Studios since CineFilm launched... no offense, darling," she said. She tossed a wicked grin at Horace. "It just took losing *what's-his-name* to speed up the collapse."

"How dare you, you over-rouged hack!" Finch shouted.

His words fell flat. No gasps. No murmurs. Not even a raised brow.

They kept on as though he were smoke curling from the old flapper's cigarette.

Across the room, the *ghostly* Vivian, the one who'd held Edmond's bloody head, arched a brow and sipped with a cruel grin.

"They can't hear you. But do go on like a jackass. I'll enjoy the theatrics," she said.

"Vivian! Hello! Horace, listen to me," Finch said.

He waved his hands in front of their faces and even shook the seated Vivian. Yes, he felt her fleshy arms in his hands.

"Ooh... looks like I've gotten a little wobbly," she said. She tried to straighten herself up. "Now be a dear and let's keep that between us, Horace. My producer is terribly sensitive when I out-drink the orchestra."

They all tittered while a waiter came through with a towel across his arm and a tray of fresh drinks.

The seated Vivian pressed a gloved hand to her lips, her eyes glittering.

"Now, now. I never drink," she said.

She paused and smiled.

"But I do *imbibe*."

"Did you really invite *him*?" the old flapper asked. "I mean Finch is so.... Finchy."

"Glory, please," said Vivian. She waved her martini like a wand, liquid splashing here and there. "Don't invoke his name. You say it three times in a dark mirror, and your soul gets optioned."

The three laughed.

"What is she saying?" Finch asked.

The ghostly Vivian drifted toward him, glass raised like a torch.

"Please tell me this isn't some grand revelation, Finch. You've known for years your name clears rooms."

Glory sniggered into her drink and tried Vivian's conjuration. "Finch. Finch. Finch!"

She paused for the sake of drama, hands cupped behind her ears like a silent film parody.

"Nope. More nothing. Just as we've come to expect."

"Good thing, too," Vivian said. "Last thing we need is summoning that wraith and losing what's left of our tipsy little Christmas spirit."

"This is outrageous," Finch said.

"Oh, darling, do shut up and listen," the ghostly Vivian said.

"You know what this party needs?" Horace asked.

The seated Vivian turned to him. The firelight caught the seams in her face, stitched together with rouge, foundation, and sheer will.

"A casting director with taste and a vermouth that doesn't settle in the mouth like mop water?" She purred the words and gave Horace a venomous smile.

Glory raised her cigarette holder in toast then puffed a cloud sideways.

Finch snarled, stepping forward. "I'm right here, you vile harpies!"

The ghostly Vivian sipped and looked bored.

"Yes, Finch. That's the problem."

"Ah, Vivian. You're a charmer," Horace said. "A snake charmer, but a charmer nonetheless."

He exhaled cigar smoke and swirled his drink. "No, what this party needs is the *other* one."

He paused, eyes searching. He stepped toward Finch and looked straight through him.

"Oh, what was his name? The *writer*... He was the witty one."

An uneasy silence spread.

The ghostly Vivian tapped her glass.

Glory rolled her eyes in exaggerated exasperation.

"Of course. The one who made that impossible man *tolerable*."

"Christmas just isn't the same without him," Horace said.

The seated Vivian coughed into her glass.

"You must be joking. He'd cut your throat to save a line of dialogue. He wasn't any better than Finch, if you ask me."

"I disagree," Glory said. "Finch was different around Malvern. Yes—*Edmond Malvern*!"

"Finch was certainly tamer," Vivian said. "Malvern helped muzzle the old bastard."

"This is outrageous!" Finch shouted. He knocked the glass from seated Vivian's hand. It clattered to the floor.

"Oopsie," she said. "Apologies, darling. Talking about the dead always makes me a bit slippery."

"I'd say you lost your grip twenty years ago," Glory said.

The ghostly Vivian now stood between her seated self and Finch.

"Now, now, Finch. You know better than to interrupt a scene in progress. Actors must *reveal* the truth. You can revise later, in your private little cutting room, as always."

Horace lifted his glass.

"Ladies. A toast to the fool who thought Finch had a heart worth saving."

The music softened. Lights dimmed. And the toast hit Finch like a punch pulled too late.

The ghostly Vivian stepped closer, her glass raised.

"Oh, we admired what you built... once. But no one does greatness alone, Finchy. You're clever enough to know that, right?"

She sipped.

"Problem is, you still won't admit what you became. And worse, you never stopped lying. Not even to yourself."

"What are you talking about?" Finch demanded.

"I suppose that's why you're here," the ghostly Vivian replied.

"And where is *here*, exactly?"

Vivian clicked her lacquered fingernails on her glass.

From the fireplace came a thick black smoke that choked the room and blinded Finch. The firelight receded and, in its place, came a much dimmer light. The clicking of Vivian's nails became the steady metronome of a clock, marking the passage of night hours.

A white whisper of fabric was all Finch heard.

He was within an enclosure surrounded by white curtains. The room reeked of cleanser and sterilized skin. Someone nearby coughed. There was a stranger on the other side of the curtain.

And Rosalind sat close. She held a young man's hand, humming a tune low and lost, small and fragile. Finch recognized it. The same as the music box: *Silent Night*.

"Oh, Timothy. My baby. My darling. *Why?*" she asked. She caressed his fingers and then squeezed them a bit. Her words sounded like prayer. But to whom? To the walls? To the bleached linoleum?

Finch's blood pounded, hard and fast.

The young man lay in the bed, swathed in gauze. He was connected to tubes and glass-domed monitors that clicked and hissed with each breath. A bag half emptied of blood hung from a metal post, feeding him through a tube threaded into his arm.

One eye on the boy was swollen shut; the other was just a slit with a red-tinted eye peering through purple lids. Blood had pooled under the skin along his jaw and neck, a slurry of brown, yellow and red. A breathing mask clouded with fog as the young man exhaled.

Finch watched the young man try to move, but his body only squirmed and deepened in the mattress. Whatever had happened, it left him as dead weight.

"Well, isn't this a festive holiday party?" Vivian asked. She stood in the corner of the bed bay, still sipping her martini.

The curtain parted, and a nun entered, gliding without a sound, as if her feet never touched the floor. Her robes were white, her bearing serene. But she radiated no grace. Whatever she resembled, it was no angel.

Finch remembered her face. Pale as frost. Silent like a forgotten church crypt. Expressionless as he'd seen her before. Now she directed her gaze to Vivian and let a smile lift each corner of her mouth.

He could see those eyes. The same ones from the morgue. Open too wide, with no glint of mercy. A barnyard pen animal's stare, blank and waiting, like the deer heads hanging in his childhood home.

Finch wanted to shout, but his voice had left him. All he could manage was a shallow gasp.

Vivian held her martini glass and reached for the I.V. stand, un-clamped the transfusion line, and let it drip crimson into her glass.

Once the glass brimmed with that dark vintage, she gave it a swirl and a sip.

"O-negative," she said. "Pairs nicely with *denial*, wouldn't you say?"

Rosalind seemed unaware of Finch and Vivian's presence. She turned instead to address the nun.

"Oh, Sister Zagan. I didn't hear you come in," she said. "Is it time for feeding?"

"Always." She let a thick tongue drop and slip across her lips. Finch widened his eyes. "But there is a man here, come to see you," she said.

"Can't he wait, Sister? I'd like just a little more time..." she said. Her voice broke on the words, and she stumbled into tears. She buried her face in Tim's side.

"May I come in?" Victor asked. He looked like he'd tripped out of bed and raced there. His hair stuck out in every direction except the right one.

Rosalind stayed buried in Tim's sheets.

"I went by your place, just like you asked. Brought you some of your things," Victor said. He held out a leather suitcase and placed it on the floor next to a chair.

Victor saw the body in the bed. He halted in place. Finch heard him controlling his voice.

"My God," he said. He stepped to Rosalind's side and placed a hand on her shoulder.

She looked up. No smile came. It was as if someone had stolen away the part of her that used to offer one with such ease. Still, she touched his hand on her shoulder.

"I also brought these," he said.

From behind his back, he withdrew a bouquet of roses.

She laid them by Tim's side. "I'm sure he would have loved to thank you..."

"I actually brought them... well, I thought you might like them. But yes. It makes sense that we leave them for Tim." He motioned toward the door, and another man in a trench coat and fedora entered but stayed out of Rosalind's line of sight. "I brought something else," Victor said.

"Oh?"

"The police came by asking questions. They couldn't find Finch. I don't know how he'd figure into all this, but... well, the detective came with me," Victor said.

The stranger in a dark suit with a gun holster strapped to his side approached.

"Good evening, Miss Crisp. I'm Officer Laraby, Los Angeles Police." He flashed his badge from his pocket and slipped it back inside. "I know now isn't exactly the best time for this..."

"For what?" she asked.

Laraby realized he still wore his hat, and he pulled it off out of respect.

Sister Zagan stepped between Rosalind and Finch and grabbed the roses.

"I'll get water," she said. She smiled, and Finch was the only one to see: teeth sharp as razors, from top to bottom.

"Rosalind... Rosalind can you hear me?" Finch asked.

"Darling, you should have that memory checked. Senescence has crept in," Vivian said. She sipped her blood, and it formed a small red wet line that ran down her chin. "I've told you already, no one can hear you. And I doubt you can still pull any more stunts by touching them.

You're well down the rabbit hole now. Now please do shut up. You're missing all the *fun*."

"Better keep my eye on that one," Laraby said. He nodded toward the nun. "I've seen hit men make more noise."

He came close and locked eyes on Tim.

"Jeez, will you look at that?" Then he caught himself. "I... I mean, he looks real peaceful-like."

"The doctors say he'll talk again. Once the swelling goes down..." Rosalind said. She braced her jaw, but tears came anyway.

"Oh, now, ma'am. I didn't mean to upset you. I was just saying how good he looks. You know... considering," Laraby said. "I can come back another time. Meanwhile, if you can remember anything Tim may have told you about his dealings with Mister Finch...."

"Mister Finch? No. Tim only did odd jobs at the studio. Mostly for me. I don't think their paths ever crossed," Rosalind said.

"Well, we've got folks who saw him leave Finch's office... just tonight."

"What? No. Why would he? It doesn't make sense."

"Rosalind," Victor said. "When I was gathering things for you, I picked up the gift from Tim that he left under the tree. Thought it would cheer you up. But I dropped it, and the paper split. And... well, look for yourself."

He handed it to her. She unwrapped it: a script and a contract. Her name was at the top.

"This was under the tree? Why, this is Finch's handwriting."

"And the tag... Tim wrote your name," Victor said. "He must have just picked it up."

"Finch would never sign me... a contract? This is impossible."

"We've had witnesses come forward. Said they observed your son leaving Finch's offices." Laraby looked at a pad he had in his pocket and read out loud. "A kid named Nathaniel Thorne. Another, elderly, called herself Adelaide. Do those names ring a bell?"

Finch's heart jammed his throat.

"No," Rosalind said.

"We got a positive identification on one of the punks who roughed up your son. We're looking for him now. Goes by the name of Frankie Boyle. Sound familiar? Did your son know him? Friends? Enemies?" Laraby asked.

Rosalind shook her head. "He said he was meeting a girl tonight..."

"Yeah. Well, Frankie and his gang are not anyone to mess around with. He and his boys have rap sheets longer than Santa Monica Boulevard. We'll catch up with them sooner rather than later. And when your son is up and alert, we'll get a clearer picture from him, too. But for now... let's just say, some of what we've heard about this Finch character raises more questions than answers."

"Questions... about Mister Finch? I mean, I knew he had a *reputation,* but..."

"Thank you for stopping by, officer," Victor said. "We'll put our heads together and see what we might remember, and we'll call you as soon as Tim is able."

Laraby leaned close to Tim's face again. "Jesus. They didn't leave much to the imagination, did they?"

Then he froze. They all stood like a film that got stuck on a single frame.

Vivian turned to face Finch, who looked on like he'd not taken a breath for the past five minutes.

"My, my my.... The police. A *reputation.* Sounds like it won't be long now, Finchy."

She gave a toothy smile, ran a finger around the rim of her glass, dipped it, and sucked the blood off.

"That's... that's a lie. I'd never really met Rosalind's son before this. She kept him hidden from me, from everyone, really. As any *normal* person would, given her friendless situation. I assumed she'd have had him sent away to be raised by wolves. Or Methodists. When he came to my office some time ago, that was the first I'd ever encountered him," Finch said.

Vivian moved along. "I seem to recall a rumor. Tim had a habit of getting chummy with the crew on the backlot... especially someone from *Vienna Tango*, isn't that so? Tsk-tsk. Such a waste. You might've gotten more use out of him... like you did the others."

Her words cut deep, but he didn't dignify her remarks with any outward sign. She swirled her glass with a lazy hand.

"These are all lies. None of this is really happening, you old harpy. It's all a twisted nightmare. And you can't convince me otherwise."

Vivian tilted her head. "Then I have an idea: *Wake up.*"

She sipped from her glass and wiped the red streak on her chin, smearing it into a grotesque blush of blood.

"Oh? What's that? Having trouble recognizing the truth?" She leaned in, smiling wide. "I say we go witness the cause of all of Tim's troubles for ourselves. A gay Christmas romp! Wouldn't that be fun?"

She splashed her blood martini in his eyes, and he shut them just as it hit.

Finch opened his eyes, and he was no longer in the hospital bed, but standing in the Rialto, a dilapidated second-run movie house with late-night showings. He and Edmond bought the place from a desperate vaudeville theater owner willing to sell it to feed his family.

It was the first of the CineFilm Finch and Malvern *theaters*. Downtown. Not a very nice part, either. The gold filagree on the ceiling peeled, and the cherubs flanking the light fixtures had nothing to say about their chipped plaster faces.

It's moonlight on the oasis,
And all I dream of is you is you...

He looked up, and there she was. Edmond's pick, not his. She had a trilling offkey quality that he detested. *Lola Fontaine*. He tried to convince Edmond to over-dub her singing. But because of the budget, they released the film with her own can-opener soprano. Audiences couldn't get enough of the girl with blonde curls and pouting lips. She batted her eyes like a sad hound begging for bacon.

The sand may shift, the stars may fade,
But I'm still wrapped in the memories we made.

A man slouching in his seat further across the expanse of the balcony mouthed the words to her song.

"She's divine, isn't she?" Vivian asked.

"What am I doing here in this... this place?" Finch asked.

"Oh, don't be such a party pooper, darling. The opening number's only started..."

"How can I be here, and the other places I've been?" Finch asked.

"Darling, you've been overdue, if you ask me," Vivian said. She sipped from her glass. "You wanted to replace her voice, remember? Just like you tried to tidy up your own little backstory. But now look at her. Queen of the queers!"

She raised her martini, and it landed like an unwarranted curtain call.

Finch scanned the balcony. All men. Just a scattering of them about the rows. Quiet movement filled the upper floor around Finch and

Vivian. Some lingered in the aisles. Some stood too close together, or sat side by side for a time then drifted apart.

A young man entered from the back through an old drape. He was slim and dark.

"I... Do I know him?" Finch asked. He squinted to see.

"Know him? Darling, add a walking stick and fleeing children, and you practically *are* him!" Vivian said.

The young man passed in front of the projection booth, and his face lit up for a moment.

"That's *Rosalind's* son, Tim," he said.

"Aren't you clever?" Vivian asked.

"Why is *he* here?"

"Why is anyone here? Because hope dies slower in the dark," she replied.

The young man shuffled in front of a group of three. He tripped and stumbled.

"Careful, sweetheart. You're not in the powder room," one said.

The others laughed.

Tim muttered a partial apology. But his voice was lower than the projector's hum.

One of the young men stood and grabbed him by the shirt.

"What did he say?"

Tim looked down and tried to peel the hand from his chest.

A patron down on the main floor shouted up toward the balcony.

"The two of you shut up."

"I wonder where I've seen them before... How about you?" Vivian asked.

Finch bristled. "I've never seen them before in my life."

Vivian lifted her martini glass and rolled her eyes heavenward. She made a graceful gesture with her free hand.

"And thus I clothe my naked villainy, with odd old ends stolen out of Holy Writ, and seem a saint when most I play the devil. *Richard The Third*, act one, scene three..." She spoke with rolls of the tongue and a doleful operatic tone. Then she took a long sip from her drink and smiled at Finch.

"Please, Vivian. I'd much rather be subjected to Lola's vocal villainies than to revisit your unfortunate summer stock performance in soggy, soggy, Ipswich," he replied.

A young man in a flat-topped service cap and brass buttoned uniform rushed in from the back aisle curtains and shined a flashlight into the row.

The young man holding Tim by the shirt let him go and patted down the wrinkles while flashing a glib smile that had no apology in it.

"It's dark in here," he said. "Someone's gonna break their neck one day."

Once released, Tim slid from the row, making his way past the usher and out.

"If only it ends there...." Vivian said.

"If he was here like the other men are here..." Finch said, "...then there are consequences for every action."

"Well, look at you, suddenly brimming with moral clarity. Should I genuflect or just bow before Saint Finch of the Back-Row Inquisition?" Vivian asked.

She placed a hand on his chest and gave him a firm push.

Finch stumbled backward, expecting to tumble from the balcony, but landed hard on the cold sidewalk.

He slammed his head against the surface behind him, hard and sharp as a snapped reel.

Tim stood nearby, fidgeting to zip his jacket. He puffed on a cigarette, lingering just long enough in the gaze of men leaving the theater. It was as though he was searching for someone.

Most pulled down their brims and passed without a word.

"Well, look who it is, Frankie," one said. "Our little balcony ballerina."

Finch watched as the young man and his friends surrounded Tim.

"Someone slip you something sweet tonight?" Frankie asked.

Tim stubbed out his cigarette and tried to edge past them.

"Where you going?" Frankie asked.

Tim kept his head down. "Hey fellas. Come on now."

"This little ballerina thinks he can pirouette past us and stroll away?" Frankie said. "Been hanging around the candy counter too long? Hungry for something?"

He unzipped his pants. His friends howled like hyenas.

"He ain't gonna find more than a gum-drop down there," one said.

"Shut up, Pete."

"Christ, Frankie, it was just a joke."

While they bickered, Tim slipped into the alley between the Rialto and an all-night diner.

"Where'd he go?" Frankie spun around.

Pete pointed.

Finch stepped into Frankie's path. He put up his arms and tried to block them. "There's no need. Why don't you just go home?"

"Come on," Frankie muttered, and he walked through Finch, who gasped with the realization that Vivian was right. They couldn't see him, and now he couldn't stop or influence any of what was happening.

Frankie sped past, picked up a loose brick, and disappeared into the alley.

Finch pressed his back to the wall. He couldn't move. A memory, vivid and engulfing, washed over him.

"You one of those funny boys, is that it? Always were soft, weren't you? Always thought you were better than the rest of us with your polished shoes and your clean fingernails. What the hell happened to you?"

The words weren't Frankie's. He was at his father's mercy again.

He was back in Harrington Vale, twelve years old, pressed to the wood-paneled wall of the sitting room.

"You think the world's got a place for boys who walk around like they're made of glass?" his father asked.

He spat on the floor, and the glob landed at Finch's feet. His face was red as a fresh welt.

"Dear, leave Bramwell alone," his mother said. She reached for his father's arm and tried to distract him. He shoved her hard. She stumbled into the furniture and crumpled to the floor.

When she sat up, she touched the side of her head. Her hand pulled away red. And part of her head looked caved in.

"Mother!" Finch said.

"You leave her out of this, you soft little nothing."

His father's voice shook. He turned to her.

"I blame you for all of this. You let him sit indoors, reading books and brushing his damn hair. You can't blame me for it. He wouldn't be like this if it were up to me."

Finch pressed harder against the wall outside the Rialto and prayed for it to end.

Pete and the other boys followed Frankie, disappearing down the alley. Their hoots and laughter warped into something sharper.

A shout, a blow. Then came a sickening thud as a body collapsed into the asphalt puddles.

"Hey!" someone shouted. "Hey! Break it up!"

It was the balcony usher. He hurried into the alley, flat cap askew and flashlight in hand.

Finch heard slapping shoe leather on the asphalt as the boys ran off and the usher tore back to the ticket booth, where he called the police.

Finch's breath caught in his throat. When it finally came, it hit strangled and strained. He turned away. He couldn't look. He couldn't see any more.

A siren sounded from the distance.

"Well. That escalated quickly. *Merry Christmas, Finch*," Vivian said. She toasted him and took a final gulp.

Finch put his hands on his knees and bent forward, trying to catch his breath and not vomit.

"Why have you shown me this?" he asked.

"Somewhere, Doctor Freud just dropped his monocle," she said.

"I'll have you know, I have no responsibility here. Why? Why was he here in this... place? It disgusts me."

"Of course it does, darling. Most things do, eventually. Your father must be burning with pride," she said. "Come now, darling. Curtain's not down yet. You wanted to know why he's here?"

The streetlamp behind them shattered in a shower of sparks, and the marquee bulbs around the theater signage exploded like popcorn until the street was silent and dark.

At the end of the dark street, close to the theater, was a single lit sign. Small, hidden just under a shingle roofline and down-lit by a bare bulb. The place looked like it tried to keep from plain sight. *The Palmetto Club*.

"Where are we?" Finch asked.

"From the looks of it, I'd say we've come to the place where romance goes to shrivel. Shall we?" Vivian asked. "But to be precise, we are about an hour before that last little gruesome vignette."

"Why am I seeing these things?" Finch asked.

"Really, darling. How long can you keep this façade going? Well, I do suppose the night is still young," Vivian said. She went to drink from her martini glass, only to find the olive rolling alone at the bottom. "Well. Even the drink knows we're past the fun part."

Glassware clinked; a jazz trio murmured low. The barkeep had sculpted the napkins with precision. The air was thick with sweet, pungent cologne that had a hard time masking gin-soaked intoxication and unmet longing.

Finch spotted Tim near the end of the bar, nursing a drink and puffing a cigarette.

The door behind them creaked open. A man stepped in. He kept his fedora low and his collar pulled up against the night.

Tim craned his neck and snubbed out his cigarette in the crowded ashtray. He smiled like he'd practiced it in the mirror, though it never came out quite right. He knew exactly how he looked but he had nothing else left in the act. His eyes flicked toward the man, dilated and still, like a creature in the instant before a car impact.

The man tipped his hat and sat at the other end of the bar. He scanned the room, peering through the smoke haze, then he removed his cloaking apparel. Another man followed behind. He was taller, a little older, and he combed his hair with care over a thinning patch. He leaned in to kiss the other man's cheek.

"Arthur! I didn't know you'd be here tonight," the first man said.

Tim sagged. Whatever hope buoyed him had deflated. He stood and went to a back booth and tried to seem invisible.

"What is this place?" Finch asked.

Vivian was in her element. A smoky room, tragic gentlemen, flickering candles, and endless gin. She smiled with an elegance that might've suited old royalty... if royalty tipped vermouth like a health tonic and savored their own tabloid scandals.

"A fine establishment, really. If you like your romance shaken, stirred, then poured straight down the drain," she replied.

She leaned over the bar and held her glass out. The bartender approached. His eyes were wrong. Too wide set. The pupils looked slitted, just like Sister Zagan's. He opened a bottle of bubbly and refilled Vivian's glass.

"How is it *he* sees you?"

"Darling, *everyone* sees me. Some of us will be remembered... and others? Well, they're only bound to become stains on cocktail napkins by morning," she replied.

The bar door opened, and a new man entered. He had a firm jaw, the kind carved out of principle, and his eyes were clear and steady, like someone who rescued children from burning buildings and never stuck around for the applause.

He spotted Tim and slid into the booth beside him, gravity nested in his shoulders, and his face carried a sorrow kept close and unspoken. He took off his hat and eased closer.

Tim managed a reluctant smile.

"You said you'd call, so I waited," the man said. He raised two fingers to the barkeep for a beer. "But when I never got the call, I figured Tim's probably at the Palmetto with something cold in his hand. And look, it's almost like I have a crystal ball."

"Look, Nicky..." Tim started. He sounded like he'd had this conversation before, like he was about to return a purchase.

Nicky turned to face Tim, but Tim averted his eyes and took a puff on his cigarette.

"Can you clue me in to whatever's going on with you? I mean, just last week we had a whole plan. You know? Margaritas? Beaches? A little place in Cabo San Lucas?"

He tried to laugh, but it came out dry and caught on a cough.

"Now I'm the idiot sitting in his apartment, checking the phone for a dial tone every ten minutes. Did I imagine something?"

"I just..." Tim said. He glanced over his shoulder, eyeing the door. "Do we have to talk about this *here*, Nicky?" His voice was low and clenched. His eyes scanned the room while he spoke.

"Last week, it was all so clear. What changed?" Nicky asked.

Tim exhaled a long ribbon of smoke, like he hoped to vanish inside the cloud it made.

"I'm not like you. I can't pretend it doesn't matter. The looks. The way people's faces change when we walk past, like they stepped on something that turns their stomachs. Like you're something to be scrubbed away."

He shook his head and continued.

"We're just built different, you know?" He took a shaky puff from his cigarette. "There are things I can't live with. And what about my mother, huh? You want me to stomp on her heart?"

"How did I not see this?"

Nicky looked at Tim like he was seeing someone smaller. Tiny, in fact.

"So, this is it, then? Hiding out at the Palmetto, waiting for something quick and quiet?"

Nicky shook his head, and Tim looked down at the ashtray.

"I never cared about the stares. I still don't. But is this really what you're trading your happiness for? A corner, a whisper, a locked door?

I can't live my life in the shadows. Not in dive bars and movie theater balconies. That kind of life? It'll eat you alive."

The door jingled. Tim twisted in his seat and tucked his lips.

The young man entering the bar was dark, slick-haired, dressed like he sold used cars and drove every one of them home. His grin was wide and careless.

Finch stiffened. "I... I know him."

"Of course you do, darling. You always did have a nose for trouble," Vivian said.

"Nicky, you have to go," Tim said.

"Ah," Nicky said. It all clicked, and his voice flattened. "Onward and upward. I see."

"Nicky, it's not like that," Tim said.

"Isn't it?"

"I can't... please don't make this harder," Tim said.

Nicky drank down the beer the bartender had just placed in front of him in three fast gulps. He slapped money down and brushed past the smiling newcomer.

The jazz trio finished their number. The jukebox whirred to life. Lola Fontaine's nasal warble of an iconic ballad swept through the room sweet and cloying as the perfume that comes free with a lipstick.

Some men sang along. Some lip-synched to Lola's words. Others raised their glasses and laughed.

The newcomer slid into the booth next to Tim and put his arm around him.

"Raul," Tim said. He didn't stand. Instead, he stared at the door as Nicky left. He looked like a man who'd seen the end of a road and finally believed it. He slid a few inches away from Raul.

"So, I was just thinking.... We skip dinner and get straight to the movies," Raul said.

"Movies? Tonight?" Tim asked.

"Yeah, I was thinking we'd head over to the Rialto. It's only a couple of blocks from here. They're showing one of Lola's finest tonight," Raul said. He whispered it in Tim's ear.

Finch tightened inside.

"The Rialto?" Tim asked. He watched the door, cigarette trembling between his fingers. He watched the door and hoped Nicky would come back.

"Meet me there in ten. You got that?" Raul asked. He swiveled out of the booth, winked, and slipped out the door.

Vivian sipped her drink. "I'm not sure I have enough octane to bear this."

"Oh, please. So, he got stood up by some dime-store Valentino," Finch said. "Happens to everyone. Are you implying that was why he was alone at the Rialto? That's why he...?"

Vivian turned. The smirk was gone.

She poured her drink onto the floor like an offering. The liquid hissed, and a hole opened where it struck. Firelight licked up from below, casting a sick glow across her features. Her smile returned, strange and stretched, lit from beneath so her eyes became pits, and her cheekbones curved into the sharp lines of a death mask.

The bar lights snapped out. The voices died mid-syllable.

The floor yawned open. It devoured the band, the patrons, and then Vivian herself.

Finch pressed to the wall, eyes clenched. Heat surged up from the depths.

All that remained was the whir and click of the projector. It sounded distant, yet impossibly near. It was as though a reel spun inside his own skull.

The heat and the projector sounds died down. When he opened his eyes, he was inside an old bathroom, with dim lights, cracked, cold, white tiles with dried yellow stains here and there. There may have been a leak somewhere, given the smell of mold and wood rot. The only noise remaining was a faucet that dripped and meted out the seconds like a torturous timepiece.

One of the stall doors hung open.

A shoe stuck out. It was one that a used car salesman might wear. There was an arm dangling down, wrist cracked on the floor, fingers curled into an agonized clench. A narrow ribbon of red ran down the pale arm, curving along his biceps and dripping one red drop at a time to the floor.

Finch felt like his throat constricted, like no words or sound could come up, and not even a drop of water could go down. His legs gave way beneath him, hands trembling as he lowered himself to the ground.

"No," he whispered. "Not... *him*."

Vivian crouched beside the body. "Oh, yes. You didn't think he'd just *disappear*, did you?"

"He was behind the scenes at CineFilm. For Lola. I knew him... I *knew* him..." Finch said. He heard the nerve gone from his voice, and he could feel himself unraveling.

"Yes. I was hoping you'd recognize your old chum. Darling, he helped with the wigs, the costumes... the magic of your personal Hollywood. Though looking at him now, I'd say the magic wore off."

"I... I never thought he'd be... be *that way*, or I'd never have had him on set," Finch said.

Vivian cocked her head. "*That way?*" She let the silence linger just long enough for it to sting.

"Oh, Finchy... And what has denial whispered this time? That he was just a walk-on from the casting pool? Some stranger drifting through the frame? Fade in, fade out, never close enough to earn a screen credit?"

She cast a glance toward the stall.

"The perfect crime, isn't it? Only let them near when you're sure they'll vanish."

His lips parted, but no sound came. Then he held his breath. He'd not crumble. That was just what she wanted from him.

"Don't drag me into this. And it's too late now, isn't it?" he said. "The man's dead. What do you expect me to do about this... situation?"

"Nothing, darling. Except what you've always done. Stand by. Let the film run. Pretend *none of it matters*," Vivian said. "Think of this little tableau as a holiday keepsake. A little memory you'll unwrap forever."

Finch felt the heat of rage spilling out from every pore. "Take me from here, if you have the power to do so. I've seen enough."

"*Enough?*" Vivian asked. "This is only the *prelude*, darling."

She slammed the stall door with her inside it, and he heard the click of the door latch.

He tried it, but it held fast.

There were murmurs outside.

"Vivian. Vivian, don't leave me here. Do you understand? There are people outside," Finch said.

"Like I said, we found this one after the guy in the alley." It was the usher's voice.

Another man spoke. "This is our second time here in a short span. Not a very good record if you ask me. I'm not sure what's going on, but I want you to work with Laraby and give him a complete description...

anything you can remember about those young men. We'll dust the place for prints, take some samples, and a few pictures for the detective."

Finch's mind spun with fear. And he froze, not knowing what he should do. The producer at CineFilm, crouched in a sleazy bathroom housing a corpse. This would end his career and would shatter his studio. His name in every trade paper and sleazy tabloid. But he was invisible to them, wasn't he?

He pressed his back to the bathroom door. Then the force of a hand pressed back.

This was no dream.

"Hey, the door's blocked," said the police officer. "Laraby, give me a hand."

Pressure built on the other side, and the door opened a crack, but snapped shut again against Finch's weight. Finch braced himself, one leg on the sink just within reach. He felt the men forcing their bodies against the surface on the other side. He wasn't a phantom. Not now. He noticed a lock fixture on the door near his elbow, which he twisted, and it snapped in place. Then he backed away.

"Did you hear that? Someone's in there. On three," the officer said. "One... two..."

He tried to sidestep, but the door blasted open, knocking him backward.

And then he was by himself. The stall and the blood, all gone. There were no straining voices of angry police.

A hallway stretched out before him. To one side, a projector ran on a table. It was the one that sat in the center of Screening Room Six. It whirred away with such intensity, he half expected it to smoke and burst into flames. The light from the lens shone down the hall. But just past the strange, disjointed images that flattened against the walls was only dimness. Tiles covered the cracked floors. Broken martini glasses lined the floors, scattered here and there. The air was cold. It was much colder than he remembered Hollywood ever being. The light from the projector changed, and the images jittered then steadied again.

Someone beyond the darkness called his name.

"Bramwell...."

ELEVEN

THE HALLWAY LIGHTS WERE little sconces, and they lit with a sudden flicker, and with each shiver of the projector's light came laughter. Not the cheerful titter of studio wives at brunch, sipping their boozy concoctions with pinkies lifted, pretending it was Darjeeling all along.

No, this was something else. It was the trill of someone who'd wandered too far from sense to find the path back.

He stepped forward, but the hallway seemed to bend to one side like a funhouse in the cold, blue, strobing light. He saw his breath coming in steamed puffs. The floor tilted to one side, and he had to hold himself upright by leaning a shoulder against a wall as he walked.

"Bramwell... Is that you?"

Her voice echoed down the darkness. It was both familiar and unwanted. He hadn't heard it in years, not since the world—his world—turned at his own hand. Sending her away hadn't erased the past. It only left him with silences reaching out from beyond to claw at him with all that was left unsaid. Always in the hushed darkness of nights that refused to end, he thought he could still hear her cries. Her anguish.

Still, there was no mistaking it. He knew her sound, though it was older now and threadbare with time. So breathy it sounded like trying to blow a feather across a dusty cabinet.

"Bramwell. I can hear you. Are you creeping down the halls?"

He heard her from a room at the end. A dim light seeped around the shut door.

Rats skittered away as he advanced, and he held his breath from the layered stench of urine and neglect.

He opened the door and saw a broken cane-back wheelchair. Someone sat in it dressed in black. She nodded and laughed, but a black veil covered her face.

"Yes... I can hear you. I can smell you. My love. My one and only love," she said.

"Mother?"

"Bramwell. Come to see what you've done? Is that it? Come to ask for forgiveness? Step closer. A mother knows when her son is near," she said.

"Can you...? Can you see me?" he asked.

"I know you're there, Bramwell! Come out! Stop playing games!" she said. She still knew how to scold, and Finch felt an involuntary, conditioned pull to follow her instructions.

A nurse dressed in a starched white uniform entered the room and rushed past Finch without noticing him there. She toted a metal tray filled with implements and a rattling bottle of pills.

"Adelaide. What are you going on about?" the nurse asked. "And why do you have that pulled over your face?"

The nurse drew it away. Finch saw his mother's eyes. They were nothing but two overgrown scars. What had she done to them? What had she *done*?

"I didn't want him to see me. Not like this," she said.

"Miss Adelaide, now, you're not making any sense today."

"My son. Bramwell. Oh, Nurse Gertrude, can't you see him? How does he look? Is he well?"

The nurse returned with a hand-stitched comforter, worn at the corners, from Adelaide's rumpled bed and covered her legs with it.

"Now, now. Miss Adelaide, you're just having a spell. Don't you see? I'm looking right now. There's no one here except the two of us." She looked over her shoulders. "You're lucky because Doctor Murr isn't making his rounds tonight and it's just me. So please, Miss Adelaide, for your own good, stop talking nonsense."

"But Nurse Gertrude, I knew he'd come for me, though I never expected it on Christmas Eve. Bramwell.... Your father is so much kinder than he used to be, that home's like heaven. He spoke so gently to me one dear night when I was going to bed, that I was not afraid to ask him once more if you might come home; and he said *yes* you should and sent me in a coach to bring you. And you're to be a man," his mother said.

"Now you'll have to stop, do you hear me? I won't read you any more of *A Christmas Carol* if you mix it all up in your head, Adelaide. Now, listen, dear, there'll be some Christmas pudding later tonight, if you can just be good for a little while longer. I hear Nurse Carver has made it extra special...with brandy in it and everything. Would you like that?" Gertrude asked.

Adelaide's mouth drooped on one side, and a line of drool slipped from the limp corner.

"Really? You'd bring me that?" Adelaide asked.

"Of course, Miss Adelaide. Now you just settle down about things that aren't true. Can you do that for your old friend Nurse Gertrude?"

"But they are true. I can sense him. He's right over there."

Adelaide pointed to her son, and he backed up against the wall.

"Now, honey. Don't ruin your Christmas. If you keep going on like this, I'll have to bring out the stinger," Gertrude said.

"I'll be good. I'll be gooder than good. I'll be goody-good. You'll see. Did I ever tell you about my son?"

"Yes, honey, you told me. He's a big movie star in Hollywood," Gertrude replied. She busied herself with stripping the stained sheets from the old woman's bed.

"No, not movie star. He's a *producer*," she said.

"Oh, he's a producer now, is he?" Gertrude replied. She sounded like she'd heard the story enough times that she could etch it word for word on her own skin. She shook her head and continued her work.

"Of course he is. He always was..." Adelaide trembled and sank more crumpled than before in her chair, as though some unseen grief, some unsaid darkness pressed her down. She spoke softer now. And slower. "He was always one to take charge... to do what was *necessary*. His father didn't think so. He was always afraid of Bramwell...."

"Who took charge and who was afraid? Honey, I'm getting lost here," Gertrude said. She folded the first sheet and carted it outside the door to a bin on wheels. She pressed her lips together, looking like she'd heard this jumble once too often.

"Did you hear that just now?" Adelaide asked.

"Hear what?"

"Was that a shot? Did you hear it, too? Of course you did. That must be Bramwell's father. He's always out there, isn't he?" Adelaide righted herself, as though better posture might jolt the darker thoughts away, exorcise them. "Even in the snow," she said. "He knows his way around the woods. You know that, don't you?"

"Honey, I didn't hear any shot. You're just not making any sense tonight, poor thing," Gertrude said.

"But you'd never hurt me, would you Bramwell?" Adelaide asked. She looked at Finch, grasped the wheelchair tires and got them in creaky motion as she rolled herself in his direction.

"Would you?" she asked. Her chin quivered, and her face melted around those gory eye gouges.

Gertrude sighed. "Now Miss Adelaide... you're just having a bad night. I think you'll feel better and have a nicer Christmas morning if you get a little sleep."

She moved with practiced quiet on the balls of her toes to the waiting metal tray. With precision, she lifted the syringe and a bottle of liquid into which she plunged the needle, never making so much as a scrape.

"Now, Miss Adelaide. I want you to be a good girl. You hear me? And you want to be a good girl, too, don't you?"

Adelaide ignored her and squeaked her wheelchair forward until she had her son pinned to the wall. His mouth gaped open.

"I always said you were a good boy. I had to, didn't I? But I never breathed a word, did I, Bramwell? Not once—even after you sent me here."

Gertrude held the syringe high, depressing it to make it squirt. But before she could plunge it into Adelaide's arm, the old woman used her palm to butt the needle up, and it rammed into Gertrude's jaw. The nurse's eyes bulged, and she gasped. Adelaide shoved her hand at the syringe again until she depressed the plunger. Gertrude folded like one of her spent sheets stripped from the beds. She convulsed for a moment and then went still.

Adelaide's scarred face softened, her torn eye sockets directed at Finch. "We'll always be together here, won't we, Bramwell? Oh, we'll have a marvelous Christmas. And we'll be happy, *won't we*?"

The nurse on the floor stirred and righted herself. Her back was to Finch and his mother. She came to an eerie stand and turned to face them. The nurse was now Vivian, martini in hand.

"My goodness, Finch. You do have a flair for touching family reunions."

She sauntered over and gazed at Adelaide, who trembled and giggled with her hands cupped to her mouth.

"Every family has its scars." Vivian toasted her sentiment and sipped. "Some are just more... *hands-on*. Finch, darling, you really know how to keep the holidays festive."

"Take me from here. I can't... I can't," Finch said. His voice broke. Pain rose thick in his throat. He swallowed hard, just to keep from letting his choking regrets consume him.

There were pieces of him he thought he'd buried for good. But now he knew darkness never stays buried, not for good.

"Oh, Finch, you're softer than chiffon and twice as wrinkled. Your father was right. One stiff wind and *poof*. It's all taffeta and tears. Pull yourself together and wave goodbye to mommy, darling. It's the least you could do after banishing her to this chamber of soft walls and forgotten screams, just like all the other memories you thought you'd hidden away. And what a gift you've left her, just like you were Saint *Nicky*. You've left her a tinsel-wrapped truth. A nightmare she can rock to sleep each night like a baby doll," Vivian said.

He took in a ragged breath and masked it before Vivian could hear.

Maybe he had told himself it was for her. He dressed up the truth as mercy, as love, or something close to it.

But after seeing her like this, he could not lie to himself anymore. His life would have been damned either way.

So, he picked the fire he thought he could stand.

But some hells burn hotter than others.

"Oh, Finchy, you weeping soufflé," Vivian said. "You're getting maudlin in your old age. Slipping, my dear. And it's undignified."

She took one last sip. "Cheers to your performance as *Son of the Year*."

Then came the sound of boots on linoleum, fast and many. The door burst open, and two orderlies in white rushed in, their faces featureless and blank as fresh-troweled plaster.

Finch tried to squirm away, but it was too late. Hands gripped his arms and forced him forward to the floor.

Vivian didn't even blink. "Oh, dear. Be gentle," she said. "This tragic little peach may still be bruised from last year's Laurels."

One of them pulled the syringe from nurse Gertrude's jaw. The others unfurled a canvas jacket with straps.

Finch fought, but the scene around him warped. The light changed. Sound wavered. His memories, all twisted together with his unvoiced pain, and then they vanished as the needle found his flesh. The scene dimmed into a black dream.

TWELVE

THE PROJECTOR RATTLED ON, frame after frame, its wheels stuttering like teeth chattering in the cold. Finch wasn't sure how long he'd been there. The darkness swallowed him, then sound pulled him back.

All he could hear was the cry of a man breaking. It was rhythmic and raw. A voice sobbed, again and again, "No..." as if it were the only word he remembered.

The screen flickered. He recognized the room. The red velvet seats. The shadowed projector booth. He hadn't left. But the room looked different now.

The seats were more tattered. The theater drapes ripped and shredding. There were cobwebs forming between the chairs.

On screen, the weeping man remained curled against the floor. He was a crumpled figure, face buried in the crook of his arm. He was rocking and repeating his broken prayer: "*No... take me from here... take me from here...*"

Finch stared, breath stopped in his chest. His heart thudded once before falling quiet. He sat alone in his theater seat, watching a man sob in the frame.

The figure rocked. Shoulders drawn tight. Still hiding his face.

He thought, for a moment, that it might be a reel from another studio. Some unseen footage that Horace might have sent by mistake.

But the scene clawed at a hidden truth. The wrongness pulsed beneath the image, cold and wet as rot.

There was no accounting for where the man in the film lay. Some dressing room, that much was clear.

The walls were black, and a single bulb swung from a wire above. Wigs and marabou feathers drooped across the chairs. A crooked rack stood along the far wall, heavy with skimpy costumes stitched in rhinestones and sequins.

Muffled music drifted in from beyond the room. *Boom-tss, ba-Boom-tss.* Slow and heavy.

Laughter followed. Rough, masculine voices climbed in volume, hooting and howling.

The projector clattered on behind Finch, manic and relentless. A shape crossed through the beam, blotting out the screen for a breath. He turned and saw Vivian with a striped, wax-coated box of popcorn. She was mid-crunch, stuffing a handful into her mouth.

"You'll have to buy your own in the lobby, dear," Vivian said. Popcorn crumbs fell like confetti from her lips.

Finch pointed to the figure on the screen. "Who is that?"

"I think the more appropriate question is, *what* is that?"

The reel ground forward. The man in the motion picture raised his eyes to the camera.

Finch didn't gasp. He only watched, unmoving, as his own face came into view. The recognition struck without ceremony. No swell of music. No grand reveal. But he felt the quiet collapse inside. Frozen chunks of denial split away from his usual armor. Tears blurred his vision. Words spilled from his lips, though he had no memory of speaking them.

"*No. Take me from here,*" he said. The line matched the Finch on screen.

He clamped a hand over his mouth as his heart dropped into the pit of his chest.

A cry broke through his fingers. It tore loose from sorrow that he'd held deep and was now unguarded. He couldn't stop himself.

"'*Overwrought*' said the Times. '*Melodramatic and insincere*', according to the Daily News. '*Far too late to change course*,' Vanity Fare raved," Vivian said. "Glowing praise, for you, really."

He heard tinkling music. It was the musical Christmas snow globe again. He lowered his hands, half-expecting to fend off one of Vivian's barbs.

But he was alone, curled on the dressing room floor he'd seen onscreen, sniffling, eyes flooded.

The music played on, small and mechanical, fighting against the reverberating drums in the next room.

Lola sat at a broken vanity, a few cracked bulbs screwed into the frame, their light weak and wavering.

The song wound down. She tipped the snow globe, twisted the key, and *Silent Night* started again. It was the same one she'd left in his office. The same from his mother's hospital. Somehow, it had found its way here.

Lola stood to secure a bra covered in a penny's worth of glitter. Her hair was a knotted mess, and her mascara melted from crying. Her boa was bald in places, the sequins on her dress rubbed dull. She took a shaky swig from a bottle of gin and fumbled with it as she tried to keep it from tipping over on the table.

"Boom-Boom, sugar, that wig looks like it crawled outta the horse stable," a woman said. She sat further away, fastening balloons to her tights. "You can use one of mine, but only for tonight, got it?"

There was a surge of music punctuating some act that got the men outside roaring.

"Ugh. I don't know what's wrong with my balloons tonight. They keep deflating in all the wrong places. Like a lotta my relationships. Still, ya gotta keep some mystery, ya know," she said.

Then she lit a cigarette and flopped onto the stool near Lola. She paused and shook her head at Lola. "Honey, cheer up. It'll all be over soon. You'll have your first real paycheck. Get some food in your stomach. The world will look a whole lot better tomorrow. Trust me. Why don't you take some of those little pills you got in your handbag? Or are you just decorating the satin lining with em?"

Lola looked at her image in the mirror and let the tears fall. "He paid me already..."

"Honey, no! That makeup won't survive two tears and a sneeze," the balloon woman said. She took a handkerchief from her purse and handed it to Lola, who looked into the mirror and tried to dab away the splotches.

"Five films. Five!" Lola said. "Then I had to open my fat mouth. Look at me. I look like a damn piñata, Busty."

"*Five films. Five films.* Is that all you can think about? Listen honey, I ain't seen a moving picture since Pickford wore curls... and do I look like I'm missin out?" Busty stared at the balloons pinned to her breasts. "Don't answer that."

Lola took a handful of pills from a brown-tinted bottle in her handbag and gulped them with whatever firewater she had left.

"Good girl," Busty said. She tied another balloon to her crotch and looked at it, satisfied. "Perfect. Gotta have reinforcements. Anyway, those little beauties you took should smooth out the rough edges tonight. And once you get into the swing of things, you can do it *aw-nach-er-al*. The performance, I mean... Besides, there's worse places you could land than this dump. I once worked a joint in Philly that had rats. And honey, they got more applause than *me*."

Lola tucked her hair beneath the stocking cap and fitted herself with Busty's poor old wig, crisp at the ends and exhausted on top. As she reached for her makeup, a glass bottle tipped. Booze pooled across the table. She wiped it up in a panic, eyes locked on the music box, as if saving it might save her, too.

Behind the women, the door burst open. A man barged in, wide as a meat truck.

"Jesus Christ, Boom-Boom! You're on next. I expected you in the goddamn wings, not gossiping with Busty and playing with a goddamned snow globe." He sounded like he knew his way around a bar fight.

She held it up. "It's Christmas, Lou. Some old blind lady gave it to me on the Red Car over here. Dressed in black, like she was headed to a funeral. Said she was going away for a long time... looking for her son. But she said I was *nice*. You hear that? *Nice*. I didn't have the heart to tell her where I was headed."

Lou stared. "Someone said you were *nice*? She really was blind, wasn't she? Now get your gin-soaked double-deckers out there and wiggle."

"For Christ's sake, Lou!" Busty said. "Give her a break. She's new."

"New? Busty, she's new like a patched-up tire," he said.

Lola tucked her lips and pressed the tinkling snow globe to her ear.

"*Silent night, holy night,*" she sang. It was so soft that the crashing drums and guffaws outside drowned it out. "You gotta understand. It's Christmas Eve, Lou. I... I can't go out there."

Lou's eyes went red. "You got paid, didn't ya?"

"I'll give it back. Every cent."

Finch watched from against the wall. Lou's face blazed like a holiday bulb about to blow.

"Yeah? When?" He picked up the bottle of hooch and tossed it into the bin, where it clanked against the empties. "Looks like you slurped it away already."

"Never you mind." She pulled up the straps of her bra and covered her cleavage with the molting feathers. "I'll get it to you."

He lunged for her and held her chin in his meaty hand.

"You're goddamned right you'll get it to me... tonight... you're gonna pick up that fan and give them a peek of Candy Cane Lane, or I swear...."

"Get your paws off me, or I'll scream," she said.

He didn't even give her a moment to think. He cranked his arm back and left her with blood spraying from her mouth. She crashed against the dressing table and cracked the shabby mirror behind her.

"Well. That's one way to bring down the curtain," Vivian said.

Finch didn't need to know she was there. The smell of a bar room clung to her like a second skin.

Vivian sipped from her glass, unbothered by what they just witnessed.

Lou advanced and clutched Lola by the upper arm, and he led her out the door.

"I must say though... the gin here's a bit *bruised*. Well, let's toddle along, or we'll miss dear Lola jingling her Christmas bells."

Finch turned to face Vivian. But twisting, he found himself seated among the men in the audience. It smelled like a sweaty locker room and whiskey breath.

The cymbals crashed, and a drum roll started. A single spotlight appeared and pooled in the center of the rickety stage. Lou came out with Lola's arm bent behind her back.

.

"We got a shy one tonight, gents," Lou said. He yanked her arm higher. "She's not modest, fellas. She's just tryin to remember which name she gave the cops last time."

The men laughed, and the cymbals crashed.

"Don't, Lou," Lola said. She tried to keep it quiet.

"You've seen her before, and tonight she shows us her 'grand re-opening.' A little saggy perhaps, but squint real hard and maybe we can all pretend it's still 1924," he said.

The cymbals crashed again, punctuating Lou's cruelty. The men groaned.

Lola whispered in Lou's ear. "Please. Don't tell them my name."

"Direct from *CineFilm* and the naughty dreams of a thousand teenage boys, I give you: *Lola 'Boom-Boom' Fontaine!*"

He flung her so she fell to the stage.

"Don't blink, boys. You might miss the last spark from this burnt-out bulb."

He left her in the lone spotlight.

The music bumped and shimmered, as if drunk on its own dim glitter, waiting for her to rise.

She trembled and tried to cover herself.

The men hooted. The band blared.

Finch shouted. "Stand up, Lola. Get off that stage. You're coming with me."

Lola placed a hand on her forehead, as if to shelter her eyes from the bleaching spotlight. She searched the audience for whoever spoke.

"Well, what do you know? She can hear you. That can only mean..." Vivian said.

"Mean what?" Finch asked.

Vivian heckled with her hands cupped to her mouth. "Too much fabric! Give the boys their stocking stuffer!"

"What does it mean?" Finch asked.

"Shh," Vivian said. "You're being rude."

Lola wobbled to a stand. One heel broken. Knees running red. Her makeup was nothing but a smear of sweat and eyeliner. She took two unsteady steps then collapsed.

The crowd murmured. Men rushed forward.

"She's dead," one of them said.

Lou came out on stage.

"Okay, fellas, break it up. Get back to your seats. She's fine. Give her a little oxygen, will ya?" Lou said.

He patted Lola on the cheek. "Come on, sugar, you're not *that kind* of dramatic."

"Boo!" Vivian said. "Give the girl her finale! More snare drum and a burial shroud!"

"Vivian!" Finch said. His voice shook, low and sharp. His fists clenched like marble knobs.

"Oh, Finchy, how noble! Making fists. I'm sure your father would think you're a real boy now," she said.

Busty ran on stage, her balloons bouncing in every direction. She slapped a syringe into Lou's meaty fist then slammed a bottle of pills into the other. One wrong word, and she looked ready to detonate.

Lou stood back. "Jesus. A goddamn junkie." He turned to Busty. "Well, don't just stand there. Have Theo call an ambulance and get yourself ready."

She rushed off, and the smoke-faded velvet curtain swept across the stage, hiding Lola's corpse.

Lou glared at the musicians. "Play something, you shitbags."

The band struck up again, as if nothing had happened.

Lou faced the crowd and tried to smile.

"Show's not over, boys! Next up we have for you a lady... and I use that term loosely... If you've got a balloon, she'll give it a blow. Give it up for Miss Busty Balloons!"

"I didn't mean... I didn't think she'd..." Finch said. He felt his heart, his lungs, his frame shrivel. "It's not my fault she was here. She was blackmailing me. I had every right to..." He heaved, and he felt his heart go dark, as though it had ever existed.

"It wasn't my fault," Finch said again. He turned to face Vivian, but she was gone. He was back in the screening room, looking at the vacant seats. Spider webs between them had doubled, and the velvet was torn away from a number of them, exposing rotting springs and felted wool. The light from the projector had changed. It sputtered, and the sprockets clicked in the way they did when the film was about to jam.

On screen, the drums rolled, and the cymbals crashed. The spotlight centered itself on the burlesque theater's curtain, and he saw it ripple. Someone was behind it, moving slow, but with measured steps. His heart found its beat again, but this time, it was thudding with horror.

A hoof scraped the floor behind the curtain, heavy and deliberate.

Then came another and another.

THIRTEEN

THE *CLICK... CLICK... CLICK* of the film reel began grinding against its sprockets. On screen, a searing white light burst through the seams of the ripped red curtain.

The images warped, then froze. The film stuttered in its track.

Finch pushed himself to standing, legs trembling, his cane forgotten.

Those hooves. Whatever was coming, it wasn't Edmond, or Nathaniel, or even Vivian. This was worse. He could feel it. *It knew him.*

He saw the front row of his screening theater littered with stiff, upright bodies covered in white morgue sheets.

"Who are you?" he asked. But they sat without moving. "How did you get in here?"

He crossed the screening room in three strides and ripped one sheet free.

He heard the hooves again, clopping out of sight. They didn't sound from the film anymore. He felt them vibrate the room. He glanced back at the screen and saw his own face warped and disfigured by an open-mouthed scream.

He looked at what was beneath the sheet.

It was burnt Nathaniel, his leaky dribbling eyeholes fixed to Finch's film-jammed screen-scream.

He pulled the sheet away from another body, and beneath was a woman dressed in black with a veil.

"Mother?" he asked.

But she sat upright, unmoving, without a single breath.

Finch yanked away the remaining sheets in the heat and impulse of rage. Beneath them were the bodies of Lola, Raul, his father, and Edmond. They all sat staring ahead, just like Nathaniel. Maybe even deader.

The projector hissed, and the sprockets jammed. The film left the reel and spooled onto the floor.

He limped to the back and tried the exit door. But it wouldn't even jiggle.

The hooves struck the ground behind him. Each step was certain and full of menace. Finch's neck locked, every tendon taught as wire. His breath stuttered in and out.

"Let me out!" he said. But no one was there to hear him. He banged with his fists on the door and repeated his plea.

The hooves continued in unhurried, well-considered steps. Up the aisle and behind him. He could feel the hot breath of someone, something.

The projector kept its gears whirring, making a mad, unstoppable sound, even as some of its internal mechanisms seemed to have malfunctioned. The light reflecting from the screen changed. It dimmed, and the room went black.

He rammed his shoulder against the door.

"Help!"

He clutched his shoulder, sharp pain radiating down as if a shard of glass had lodged there. He took desperate gulps of air.

The door swung open on its own. Beyond it, Finch saw Nathaniel's barn burning from the inside. It was a catastrophe of flames and smoke.

"Nathaniel! Nathaniel, are you there?" he asked.

His lungs filled with hot soot, and he bent forward, retching liquified smoke.

The only answer was the crackle of flame and the groan of the collapsing rafters.

From the burning haze, Finch saw it emerge.

It was white all over and well-groomed everywhere except for its chest and mouth. Legs that bent in the wrong direction and horns, four of them grown in crooked spirals that crowned its head. He'd glimpsed it that terrible day and saw it up close in the barn when it tried to ram him. It had waited in the wings at the Palm & Pearl Club. It peered from mounted deer heads. It was as if it was always there, watching, haunting him, across his whole life and maybe before.

It stood erect and folded its strange shorter arms and clawed hands where front hooves should be. They were stubby things with sharp nails, cracked and split on each of its three fingers. It chewed on food. Whatever it munched stained its mouth and surrounding pelt red. Deep red. Some of it dried and caked.

The animal clopped forward across the doorway as Finch backed away and stumbled in the dark over the chairs. It entered and loomed over him. A foul musk radiated from the creature, an acrid blend of barn animals and spoiled meat.

"Who... who are you?" Finch asked.

The animal advanced several commanding steps and turned its head so its slitted eye on one side could better account for what it saw.

It bleated and sounded like its cry was almost a shouted word.

"Whoo-o?" it said. "Whoo-o?" Finch saw in its skin-crawling attempt to speak, it curled its lips, revealing rows of pointed saw-teeth. Rows and rows of them, where teeth never belonged. It continued to chew, and from its mouth, a bloody finger fell.

Finch backed into the wall, ribs locked, lungs unmoving. The goat's unnatural voice passed through him like a decree from a forgotten god, each shaking syllable searing into his soul as if this moment had roots in destiny.

"Leave me! Leave!" Finch cried. His voice had climbed beyond panic and was one tick below admittance to an *Asylum for the Utterly Insane*.

"Le-eee-eeve," the creature said. Its voice shivered like a broken incantation, part animal, part echo. Nothing human.

"God in heaven! Help me!" Finch said.

"He-e-e-lp!" the goat said.

A strand of saliva dripped from its maw, slim and bloody. It pooled on the ground near Finch. He recoiled.

"What... what do you want?"

The corpses of his past remained upright and rigid, staring at his contorted image on the screen. Finch felt their silence press in on him, heavier than condemnation. He couldn't look at them long. Not when he knew what he'd taken.

His voice escaped like a final breath. "I can't undo the past."

The goat resumed chewing, and it watched.

Finch wanted to close his eyes, but he dared not.

"And what would you have me say?" he asked. His voice collapsed into the words he dared to utter but perhaps should not have.

"What more do you want from me? What more is there to see?" Finch asked.

"See-ee," the goat said. Its eyes pointed in opposite directions, wide and glassy. There was no kindness behind them, no reason, only the cold, unblinking hunger of every soul that had never once felt the need to understand. They were vacant of everything except impulse and appetite.

Panic seized him. He turned to run, but the creature was already there, chewing with its buzz-saw teeth. Finch doubled back and lurched through the door from which that unspeakable beast had come. Sparks and embers still swirled through from that place behind the door. That other time where regret took root.

He landed face down in wet grass. The sky was gray, and the air smelled of recent rainfall. He stood and tried to wipe away mud and green blades that were stubborn and clung to his clothes.

There were people gathered, dressed in black. He stumbled forward.

No one spoke. They just stood there, eyes fixed on the canvas-covered mound, as if unsure whether the grave would hold what they'd left buried. A minister in a purple stole read from a small black book, but the words never reached Finch's ears. They arose and dissolved as nothing more than breath fogging up the winter air.

There were twenty in all. There wasn't anyone he could call a friend. They were all CineFilm employees. They stood with the appropriate faces, as though dictated by a memo: somber and drawn as they surrounded the rectangular mound. The minister shook an aspergillum, flinging droplets at the pile.

Finch saw himself there. He was more crumpled than ever. Whatever his age, he looked twice it that day. He wore a top hat, a black wool suit, and a cravat fastened with a ruby stickpin that gleamed like a drop of sparkling blood. He clutched a rain-slicked umbrella as if it were the last object tethering him to safety.

The minister spoke Edmond Malvern's name then followed with the expected words and prayers, scripted sentiments meant to honor the dead and to warn the living.

Finch remembered that day. He remembered those faces. Those practiced faces that required a day's pay to attend Malvern's graveside service.

"Why am I here?" he asked. He knew the goat, that sickening creature, had to be somewhere nearby.

"Why-yy-ee?" it bleated.

He knocked on the door with a hand that was firm and unblemished. Despite the rippled glass meant to obscure his view, he could always see enough to know if the instructor was in.

"Yes, yes, come in Finch," Horace said.

Finch opened the door and saw Horace V. Bellamy sitting behind his desk. A mountain of canisters loaded with 35-millimeter film rested on his desk. It was all lit by a lamp that gave everything in its wake a sepia-tone.

The acetate from some of the film reels curled just enough to hint they might have good stories to tell. Just as likely, they had ones worth forgetting, especially if they were from first-year attendees of Horace's filmmaking salon. To young Finch, the reels and scripts piled on Bellamy's desk weren't clutter; they were hope. Bellamy was still looking. Still open.

The elder Finch was in a corner of the room watching his younger self eye the master. What was coming, he knew. Turning away was out of the question. He knew what he'd find, just waiting to take him. He could smell that blood-soaked pelt.

Bellamy boomed like Santa Claus at a holiday parade. "Well, don't just stand there, boy. In this business, silence is always the wrong choice. And I won't stand for gawking."

"I... uh... I thought you might like this."

Young Finch placed a manuscript bound by a cardboard binder onto Bellamy's desk, and he backed away.

"Ah yes, I remember you now. The eager boy with the sob story disguised as cinema. What was it you screened that put the entire salon of thirty to sleep?" Bellamy asked, exhaling smoke into Finch's face. "Christ, I should've had my head examined for picking some of you," he muttered, eyeing the manuscript. "I don't read pages from boys who think opening with a dead mother and ending with a violin solo counts as cinema. Come back when you've got something that doesn't whimper... or double as a sleeping aid."

Finch watched his younger self go pale. He cleared his throat and tried again. "I'm sorry sir. This... this script isn't mine. But I thought you might read it."

"Read it?" Bellamy roared. His face turned purple with his guffaws. "You think I'm going to read something handed in *from you*?"

He laughed harder and choked on phlegm. Finch shrank a bit. Bellamy continued.

"Cocky and delusional. A combination that's only good for government work. Good day, Mister..." Bellamy said. He squinted at the boy, and it was clear he'd forgotten his name.

"Bramwell."

"Fine, Mister Bramwell. *Class dismissed*," Bellamy said. He lit a cigar and puffed it to life like he was born with nicotine in his blood.

"No... Finch. I'm... Bramwell Finch," he said. The elder Finch watched himself stutter, and he could remember how strained his throat felt, how small he became in Bellamy's presence.

"Yes. Well, Mister Finch. You didn't seem to know much about exits in your short film, so let me direct you this time: the door is right behind you," Bellamy said.

Finch advanced and braced himself on Bellamy's desk.

"If you will, sir. It's called *Moonlight Over Morocco*. If you'd just take a moment and read. I'm sure you'd find it... satisfactory."

"Satisfactory?" Bellamy scoffed. "Son, you seem to have trouble reading the room. Here's a tip: Go home. And when you get back to Dusty Pines or wherever it is you've wandered in from, check if the local diner's hiring. At least there, someone might order up what you're serving."

"I was hoping you might produce it, sir," Finch said. He stood firm. If the room burst into flame, he'd burn before stepping back.

Bellamy chuckled, like he was waiting for a better punchline. "Produce it? Finch, did you hit your head on the way in?"

Young Finch set a manila envelope on the desk with deliberate precision.

Bellamy raised an eyebrow. "What's this?" He slit it open then stopped. The sight of crisp hundreds stacked inside killed his laughter.

"Where'd this come from?" he asked.

"My father."

Bellamy glanced up. "Don't tell me he's in the mob."

"Preston Aldridge Finch."

Bellamy blinked. "*Railcars-and-steel* Finch?"

The youth nodded once.

Bellamy leaned back and paused. He gestured for Finch to shut the office door. He held up the script with one hand and the envelope of cash in the other. "That's the smell of culture, boy: fresh ink and old money."

"The papers said your last picture cost forty thousand. That's fifty. Up front. You're already in the black."

Bellamy thumbed the bills like he was getting reacquainted with an old lover.

Finch continued. "And sir, if you're still not sure, read the script. It's a real humdinger...."

"This does all the talking," Bellamy said. He fanned the bills. Then he tossed the envelope on the desk and grabbed the manuscript. "I think we should give your old man his money's worth."

"I remember that day," the elder Finch said.

He knew the creature listened. Its hot breath, redolent of barnyard and death, washed over him. He heard it taking its throaty breaths and snorting through its blood-stained nostrils.

"I knew I could do this... make Edmond into something. And, if all went well, he and I could build an empire. I wouldn't let anything or any*one* stand in our way."

He remembered the way Rosalind looked at Edmond in the library that same day. She was so open, so sure. He remembered Edmond's plan to propose and the ring box in his pocket.

He was no fool.

He remembered how he'd stepped between them, armed with charm, urgency, and that contract from Bellamy.

It was a perfect interruption, timed to the second, like any good production.

Back then, he told himself it was only business. That was the lie he could live with. But even then, he knew what was behind it all.

The creature placed its strange little hand on his shoulder, and he could feel its nails sink into his skin. Not hard enough to puncture. But they landed with the sting of a warning.

FOURTEEN

THE SCENE SHIFTED AGAIN. Finch saw himself, older now, no longer a college boy. Young enough, though, that there was still some polish to him. He'd already taken to wearing a black suit now that Cinefilm was well on its way to making its mark.

He stood outside a familiar apartment. It was cold, the sky bruised with winter. Rain had fallen just yesterday, and puddles reflected the red of passing trolleys.

"I come bearing gifts," Finch said.

Flour smudged her apron. And her cheek, too. A fine dusting of white caked her hands. She wiped her forehead with the back of her wrist, just missing the scarf she'd knotted around her hair. Rosalind noticed the gift-wrapped box in Finch's hand, and she turned her back on him, returning to her kitchen task, leaving him to stand by himself within the open door.

"Just leave it on the table. I have a lot on my mind," she said. She didn't bother turning toward him to say it.

The older Finch watched. "I remember this," he said to the creature. He knew it listened. "Why must I see it again? I only did what was necessary." The creature snorted through its flared nostrils.

Finch went on. "You don't make history by preserving the past. When shining cities rise, no one blames the wrecking ball for doing its part."

He heard the words and felt them falter, even as they left his mouth. Still, once upon a time, they had been enough to sleep by.

"I came to offer you a job," younger Finch said.

"A job? I already have one. Production assistant. Remember? Thanks, though," she said. She looked at home in her simple kitchen while she turned a wooden spoon around the edges of a big, powder blue bowl.

"A directing job."

She set the spoon and the bowl down.

"You're teasing me. You're just being mean.... So, is this little visit just to ruin my Christmas? Well, you can run along now that you've had your laugh," she said.

She turned her back to him and opened a cupboard, removing an amber bottle. She unscrewed the top and poured some in the bowl.

"It's no joke," Finch said. "Open the box."

She locked eyes with him for a moment then wiped her hands on her apron. Making her way around the counter, she found the box on the entry table. Finch stayed where he was.

She tore the wrapping paper away and let it drop to the table then marched back toward him, holding up a silver rattle like she meant to ram it down his throat.

"How did you know?" she asked. Her voice cracked like dry kindling. Her cheeks flushed, lit from within.

"Rosalind, don't be a fool. I've seen you on set, sick, pale, green for weeks. The retching. The fainting. It's obvious."

She stumbled back and dropped into an oversized chair, her body collapsing like a marionette with its strings cut.

"Jesus." She pressed her hand to her face. "I never meant for this to happen. You know? I never...."

Finch softened. "Of course you didn't. And now you need help...
and that's why I'm here."

Rosalind looked through her fingers. "Help? I thought you were
offering a job."

"I am. Listen," he said. "Our next picture's set in San Francisco.
Shadows in Chinatown. I want you to take point on the atmospheric
scenes. Foggy alleys, trollies, the bridge under construction. You'll get
assistant director credit. And that should be enough to open doors.
You could write your own ticket after that."

Older Finch watched Rosalind's face change. Her panic returned.

"But it will be obvious in time. People will see. And then they'll talk.
That would ruin me... ruin my career. You know better than anyone,
if word got out...."

"And it won't," Finch said. "You'll go for principal filming then
stay on with a skeleton crew. It'll just be three of you. No press. No
fuss. I'll set you up with an apartment, and you can vanish for the
months following that. Tell the crew that you fell in love with The
Embarcadero and can't live without Fisherman's Wharf."

"This is crazy," she said. "How would I live?"

"Too bad you don't know anyone with money," he said. "Did you
look under the rattle?"

She creased her brow and returned to the box, parted the tissue
paper, and pulled out an envelope thicker than a deck of cards.

"That should last you through the end of the year. Maybe longer,"
he said.

"But my life is here. The studio, Edmond... you. What would I do
with a baby in San Francisco?" she asked.

"Live your life. Lie low," Finch said. "Once enough time's gone by,
you'll reappear and pick up where you left off. *Shadows in Chinatown*
will have shown, and you can take advantage of your new screen credit.

And as far as the baby..." He hesitated, choosing his words. "If anyone asks, you can always say it's your sister's. And I'll vouch for you."

"But Edmond... he deserves to know," she said.

"Rosalind... I seem to recall you once said you wanted whatever would make him happy."

He studied her. "Have you read his latest draft of *Dusk Over Savannah*? It's Edmond's greatest work. You know what happens once it premieres. The man is on the cusp of everything he's ever wanted. You know what that feels like. I saw your eyes when I offered you the directing job."

He leaned in. "But if he knew about the baby... you think he'd let this all go by like passing scenery? He's too decent. He'd give it all up. And if he sets aside his dream to disappear into a little house in the Valley, tucked behind the orange groves, with a crying baby and nothing but a box of old newspaper clippings and yesterday's promise...?"

Finch paused and looked into Rosalind's eyes, and he watched her hope evaporate.

"How long before that sacrifice sours? You'd be living with a man who saw his life as a trap. You're smart, Rosalind. What do men do when they feel trapped?"

Her eyes brimmed over. She wiped them with her sleeve.

"You're right."

"I only want this for you. I only want this for your child," Finch said. His voice was seductive. "I'll be there for you. I promise." He pushed the envelope toward her. "And once his film is made, once his future is secure, you can step back into the picture and make things right again. In the meantime, I'll see that you have everything you need."

The elder Finch watched himself and felt his excuses, his defenses tear his insides. It began small then split wider, like a fault line shaken by what lay buried beneath.

He glanced at the creature, which stared with its wide black eyes. It chewed again, slow and purposeful, like it dared Finch to look away. A thread of wine-dark fluid slipped from its mouth and splattered to the ground. Finch kept still, though his stomach turned.

"She did as she was told. Went to San Francisco. Why wouldn't she? Tim was born that December. The crew had left months before. She was alone...."

He tried to swallow, but it stuck.

"Her son came five weeks early. I... God, it was perfect. The break I needed. No more justifying. She couldn't leave, not after that."

He stared down.

"I sent roses. Money. Enough to keep her there. Enough to keep her...."

He felt the small, sharp nails sink into his shoulder again. Deeper this time, clean and deliberate. He didn't cry out. He understood.

"I knew I could bring her back. Just the same as I sent her away. But I couldn't help myself," he said.

"*He-ee-lp*," the goat said. The sound trembled, half animal, half word.

When Finch winced, the scene had already changed.

"I believe this calls for one more," Finch said.

He raised a green bottle capped with foil.

"No, Bramwell, enough," Edmond said. He laughed. "All right, one more."

"Of course, one more! A thousand more! Do you know what tonight means? Do you?" Finch said.

He poured for both of them. The driver turned to the right, and champagne spilled across the floor.

"Careful, Bramwell. You're wearing half the bottle, and we haven't even stepped out. There'll be cameras, you know. The driver can't see, can he?"

Finch handed the full glass to Edmond and raised his own in a toast.

"Nonsense," Finch said. "He can't see or hear anything unless I page him. Look here..."

He pressed a button near Edmond's head. The partition cranked down.

"Yes, sir?" the driver asked.

"Oh, Samuels. Will you take us to the theater by way of Fountain Avenue?" Finch asked.

"Of course, sir. Anything else?"

"Yes, that's all, unless you stumble across another case of champagne on the curb. Then, by all means, stop."

The partition cranked back up, sealing the two men and their conversation away.

"Are you sure we should have sprung for this limousine?" Edmond asked.

"Oh, more of your accounting hogwash," Finch replied. "What do you expect the reporters want to see? The producers of *Dusk Over Savannah* arriving in a horse-drawn carriage? Now hold your glass up so I can properly toast."

Edmond did as he was told but looked at Finch the way one might a naughty child.

"To the success of *Savannah*. May she sweep the Laurels as she so richly deserves," Finch said.

Their glasses met with a hearty clink, but Edmond didn't sip like Finch. He lingered for a breath. He smiled a kind of warm, unguarded grin one doesn't plan, but that changes the moment.

Finch had spent months planning, scheming, obsessing over every detail. His focus tightened his scope of awareness so tight he didn't notice until now how close they'd grown.

And then Edmond winked.

A flash overcame Finch. Then it was gone as quick as it arrived. But Finch felt it, and it rattled him. He laughed loud, brushing off whatever ugliness, whatever tremor, whatever burned beneath the surface, as though it was a tickle from champagne fizz. It was nothing at all. Nothing.

The elder Finch sat next to himself in that back seat. The goat watched him from across, sitting right next to Edmond.

"I told myself it was nerves. Nerves and nonsense and too many interviews," he said.

The goat clasped its strange sharp little hands, one atop the other at its chest, and cocked its head so it could better size Finch up.

The younger Finch tossed the drink back faster than he'd intended.

Edmond followed suit, gulping his own down with a grin.

"You really made it all happen, didn't you?" Edmond asked.

Finch thought he might choke. He coughed and held a hand to his throat. He fiddled with the champagne bottle, twisting the foil, resetting the glasses. His heart gave a slow, stupid thump.

"Well, it took us both, I believe," he said. "We're CineFilm now, remember? Finch and Malvern Studios. Immortal. Unkillable. Practically gods."

He kept his gaze down, afraid Edmond might see in him the vulnerability, the awful weakness he hadn't meant to show.

"Practically," Edmond said. But he spoke his words like a song. Or Finch had never noticed before how musical Edmond's voice was before this.

Finch felt Edmond's steady eyes on him, the curve of his grin. It landed with a weight he didn't know how to carry. Friendship. Or more. Or less. Brotherhood, maybe. Something he'd never earned from another man before.

Finch closed his eyes, and he was standing in the forest surrounding Harrington Vale. He was sixteen again. He didn't want to see it again. But it never stopped playing. It was like a phonograph record that never ended.

"Still playing at being a man, Bramwell?"

He could see his father's cool fury.

"You think you're going to prove that you're not as soft as chiffon? Go back home. It's Christmas Eve. Run along, put on an apron like a good lad, and make sugar cookies with your mother," he said.

Bramwell never intended it. But he couldn't help it. His father had never wanted him, never needed him. Never loved him.

The forest stank of damp pine and smoke that Finch could still remember. The air held that silvery tension it does before a lightning strike. Bramwell felt the cold of the shotgun barrel in his hands, heavier than he thought. His father refused to let him use it. Said he'd only shoot his own foot or worse, that a boy like him had no business holding something meant for men. But it was in Bramwell's hands now, and he was a man. It had been resting against his knee just moments before.

His father turned away, cursing under his breath about sons who talked like stenographers and who folded napkins better than they held long guns.

The trigger pulled itself. That was what Finch would say to himself from that day forward. No one saw otherwise. No one else knew.

The blast echoed like a thunderclap, cracking the sky open and the valley in half.

Finch dropped the gun before his father hit the ground. Before the birds screamed and hurried for shelter. And before the steam of breath stopped seeping from his father's open mouth.

He knelt and watched him. The small crust of snow swallowed his blood. The birds watched from the branches above and were silent now.

"You... you shot me," his father said. His eyes looked like he was pleading.

"Yes," Bramwell replied. He felt his heart. It ached. Un-beating. Unmoved. What he'd done did not heal as he thought it might.

"Get... help..." his father said. But his words were more like bubbling gasps of air.

"No," Bramwell replied.

"You... you... killed me...."

His father's eyes were still now, and his chest stopped moving.

"Yes," Bramwell said.

He picked up the gun and crunched away in the snow, shoulders held back. He was a real man now. A hunter, just like his father wanted.

And when Finch opened his eyes, he was in the limousine once more. His face was close to Edmond's. It was too close. Their knees touched. He could smell the sharp citrus of Edmond's aftershave and the sweeter trace of champagne in his breath.

He didn't pull away. And neither did Edmond.

Finch felt time stop, and he felt as though the silence between them pulsed like an overused telephone wire. He blinked, unsure of how long he'd been staring.

"I've noticed something, and I'm not sure you would approve..." Edmond said.

Finch felt his whole mouth run dry. He wanted to say something. But there were no words.

Edmond came a bit closer. Finch shifted in his seat. He could feel the color drain from his face.

But Edmond didn't react. He moved in.

"I saw this," Edmond said. His fingers reached toward Finch's collar and tugged.

For a second, Finch realized he couldn't find his breath.

"Lint," Edmond said. He inspected it between two fingers. "Hardly red carpet-worthy."

Finch chuckled, but the sound was not himself, and he tried to cover the pinched sound with a cough.

"There," Edmond said. He leaned back in his seat. "I just rescued you from the disgrace of an imperfect collar. The tabloid photographers can thank me later. So, I assume I don't owe you anything anymore for this magic carpet ride into our future."

Finch turned away and gazed out the window, but he felt the ghost of that touch still tingling on his neck. Or perhaps it was deeper than that.

The driver pressed a button that buzzed in the back seats.

Finch rolled down the divider between the back and front. "Yes, Samuels."

"Shall we take the alley to the theater door? Or would you like to arrive out front?"

"Out front, Samuels. From this day forward, out front."

Edmond smiled. He turned to the window, watching the glittering lights and crisscrossing searchlights. Then, without warning, he reached across and pushed Finch back into his seat.

Finch felt the heat of Edmond's broad hands, the strength behind them.

"Looks like a full house tonight," he said.

Then he reached across and touched Finch's knee. "...And you, Bramwell, look like you've been swimming in bubbles since noon. Let's hope the photographers can give you some grace. And for God's sake, don't stumble."

Finch shifted, brushing at his lap, though nothing was there.

"Should've kept the lint," Edmond said. "Might've distracted them."

Finch straightened himself, pretending to adjust his cufflinks, smoothing his hair with a damp palm. His throat burned like he'd crossed a desert with no canteen.

The ghost of his father still lurked in the back of his mind, hissing, "I should've drowned you at birth. Would've saved us both the shame of this pantomime."

But Edmond didn't know about that. And he didn't shrink back like Finch.

The elder Finch watched the scene, heavy with words left unspoken. Silence wandered its way through him like a restless ghost searching through dark halls for what it might have left behind.

"I don't seem to remember this..." the elder Finch said. But even as he whispered the words, he felt them damning him.

The goat shuddered out a half-word. "Rrre-mem-berrr." Its voice sounded like a film getting shredded within the sprockets.

The studio offices had emptied hours before this. Only the hum of old desk lamps and an intercom with questionable wiring remained.

Edmond loomed in the doorway, his coat slung over one arm.

Finch didn't look up from the pages in his hand, but he adjusted his spectacles.

"These are your notes on Lola's wardrobe?" Finch asked.

"We'll talk about it tomorrow. It's an expense we can do without. Anyway, I'm beat. It's midnight, and we start principles tomorrow morning at five," Edmond replied.

Finch smirked and raised his eyebrows. "Huh! Soft as chiffon. I remember an Edmond who'd stay up all night with the reels."

Edmond eyed Finch and walked toward him with a quiet tread. He placed a folded envelope on top of the script. "This is something else I think you should read."

"What is it? Is this from our lawyer? I knew he'd be useless for our distribution mess."

Edmond laughed. His face was radiant. Strong.

"It's definitely not legal, Bramwell. Christ, is everything the studio with you?"

"Yes. And it isn't for you? No wonder we're short on Laurels."

"Look, I got it from someone who wants to stay anonymous. Says bringing it to you might make things more complicated than they need to be. So here. Just read it, will you?" He hesitated and nodded in time to some rhythm only he could hear. "Tonight. Will you?"

Finch glanced at the envelope but didn't touch it. "You're not quitting, are you?"

Edmond shook his head. "Jesus, Bramwell. You're going to give yourself a heart attack. I'm not quitting. Good night."

He left before Finch could say another word.

Finch stared at the envelope. There was something in the handwriting, and in Edmond's tone, his manner. It was all just enough to unsettle. He slipped it beneath a stack of paperwork, but after a moment, he pulled it free and locked it away in his desk drawer.

The goat stepped to the elder Finch's side and gestured to the desk. Like a cruel magician, it produced the key from nothing but the air. It held the little brass thing between its split-nailed claws.

Finch held his breath against his memory, but it came anyway. It crawled through the locked rooms of his mind like some unnamed horror unleashed. He took the key, knowing the consequences were already set in motion. Yes, he took it, but even as he did, he felt his heart shrink against a tidal wave of truth. The drawer had been locked for years, the note inside untouched. Finch had kept it that way for a reason. Once read, it could not be undone.

The goat stared at him, and he knew it was time. He opened the drawer, and there it was. He removed the envelope... the very same that had arrived with Edmond's clothes from Saint Cyprian's morgue. He read the typewritten message.

> *I don't know how else to say this. The secrecy and the pretense can't go on. If I'm wrong, forgive me. But if I'm right, we've both known for far too long and haven't fulfilled what we need to do. Please come tonight. It's time we did this together.*

The note fluttered from Finch's fingers and burned, curling into gray ash before it touched the floor.

"I wouldn't allow it. I... there was too much at stake. Oh, my god... Edmond. All I gave him was my drawer...."

He buried his face in his hands. Tears long locked away found their way out, bitter and stinging. But the goat was undeterred. Its hideous claws clutched his shoulder and sliced through his skin, burrowing deep into the marrow of his regret.

Finch sat alone in the screening room. An old reel with Lola belting in that pinched, theatrical voice broke the stillness. Projector light bathed the room in the gleaming white that reflected from her shimmering gown.

"Christ, it's like listening to a goose getting strangled," Finch said. He knew he was alone, but her voice had the power to unravel him.

He snubbed out his cigar into a nearby free-standing ash can.

"It's official. After this, I'm billing the studio for pain and suffering. But right now, I'll take it in whiskey...."

He heard a forceful knock.

"Come in, Hank," Finch said.

A small man entered, his thinning hair slicked back, his glasses capable of focusing sunlight into a blaze. His voice shook.

"Mr. Finch, we've looked at everything. The final tally's in."

"And?"

"It's gone, sir. All of it."

"Gone..." Finch said. "I guess I shouldn't have wasted this." He picked up the cigar and looked to see if he might salvage it.

"Sir, it's like everyone else's. We're all wiped out, sir. Even some banks are going under. I had my savings at the *Commonwealth Trust & Mercantile*, but they told me I couldn't take anything out, not now," Hank said. "This is just terrible, Mister Finch. People are jumping from high-rises. It's the end of the world, I tell ya."

"Now, Hank. It can't be all that bad," Finch said.

"Oh, yes, sir. It is. There's chaos in the streets. And just how will I pay my ex-wife now? My apartment?"

Finch stood and put his arm around Hank's shoulder.

"As long as you stay with CineFilm, you'll always have Millie's payment," Finch said. "And Hank, don't get married again, will ya?"

Hank nodded and held his visor in his hands. "Yes, sir. And, thank you, sir." He turned to leave.

Finch had a hunch this financial devastation was coming. Hell, Babson had screamed it from the rooftops just the week before, and it was all over the papers. And the Reserve kept hiking interest rates. It was inevitable, though few considered it. They wanted the party to keep going. But he had tucked away enough in the walls of his house and in the CineFilm vault to keep the company breathing, just in case. And if it came to the worst, well, he'd be fine while the rest of them wheezed into ruin.

A tip from the devil himself, he thought. Not bad. His suspicions were all speculation at the time. But those instincts, the same ones that had saved him a thousand times before, paid off. CineFilm could have its chance now to rise to the top of the industry. The rest of them, Bellamy and Carrington Black, would be the executive producers of crumbling façades and vacant back lots. But not Finch.

Edmond pushed past Hank and entered the screening room. His hair looked like he'd had his hat torn off in a cyclone, and his necktie was loose and askew.

His forehead dripped.

He threw an envelope down onto the small table between the theater seats where Finch kept his script and a cocktail. It landed with a slap.

"I was looking for a script copy and found this below a whole stack on your desk. It's stuffed with bills," Edmond said. He spoke like he was out of breath.

"How touching, Edmond. You know how I love money," Finch said.

"You think this is funny?" Edmond asked. "You think a Christmas card for Rosalind... and *her boy* stuffed with money is a joke? A thousand dollars. A *thousand* dollars? Why?" Edmond asked.

Finch took a sip from his drink.

"Well, 'tis the season, as they say." His lips pressed to the rim of the glass, as though he needed the drink to suppress a nervous laugh.

"Don't do that," Edmond said. His cheeks burned, not from shame but from a building fury. "You can't just laugh this off."

"She needed money. I gave her money. Is there some harm in that?"

"Tim has gray eyes. And a cleft chin. Blond hair," Edmond said. He pinched a tuft of his own hair. "The same as mine." His voice faltered then steadied. "I'd seen that before while he was on the back lot. I always wondered about it but shrugged it off as coincidence. But then I remembered. Rosalind went to San Francisco... and she stayed gone. No letters, not a single word. And when she came back, she had this kid. She told people around the studio that he was her sister's. But Rosalind never had a sister. I never said anything because it was none of my business...."

"And there I agree with you," Finch said.

"Did you think I wouldn't figure this out... once the boy started becoming a man? You think I'd never *notice*...?"

"Good grief, Edmond," Finch said. He swirled the drink in his hand. "It's clear who the writer is between us. If only you'd put this much effort into one of your scripts...."

"Goddammit, Bramwell. I can just ask her, and she'll tell me, you know. She'd never lie, not to me. Admit it: you paid her to disappear back then. Didn't you? Why?"

"Edmond, I'm not sure what you're driving at. Rosalind made a graceful exit during... a *compromising* moment. She knew she couldn't afford the gossip. And the more I thought about it, neither could CineFilm. Haven't you heard the moralizers on the radio? Everything is *sinful* these days, especially Hollywood. So, can you fault me for helping her? She asked to keep it quiet, and I honored her request. But now... congratulations. You've unearthed her little secret." Finch raised a shushing finger to his lips.

"Whose kid is he?" Edmond's voice trembled, not with weakness, but with the struggle to keep words he'd later regret to himself. And the words he did let loose landed like a match head, ready to ignite.

"Why don't you ask her then?" Finch asked. "Go dig it all up. Let's see what the truth will cost her *this time*, shall we? Go drag her through a painful encore. I'm sure she'd be thrilled to relive what she's *obviously* wanted buried for years now... all for her own reasons. Shame. Guilt. A misstep that she corrected. Or maybe she kept it out of sight because if it got out, she'd be ruined... I had no idea how heartless you were, Edmond."

With a sweep of his arm, Edmond struck the glass from Finch's grip. It shattered across the floor in a punctuation of crystal and fury.

"I want to hear you say it," Edmond replied. His voice was lower now. Honed. Every syllable, a blade.

Finch sat unmoving except for the quiver in his jaw. His breath halted, and for a moment, he couldn't lift his eyes from the shards scattered and reflecting the projector light like a hundred accusations. But the words he'd buried, those words that were too sharp-edged and dangerous to let loose, pressed against his tongue. He tried to bite them back, but they rose anyway.

"It was all for you, Edmond. She did it all for you. She knew you'd pitch your whole career aside, and she didn't want you to blame her in time."

"No." Edmond shook his head. His voice grew stronger. "You *told* her to go. I know you. You think I don't? You probably told her my career would collapse. That CineFilm relied on me. Didn't you? Didn't you?" His eyes were glassy, and tears trailed down without shame.

Edmond stood over the shards of Finch's shattered cocktail glass, his chest heaving. "People were right about you," he said. "I tried not to listen. I tried to tell them otherwise. I gave you *excuses*. But it was true... and you *even did it to me*. You stole..." Edmond struggled against the surge welling in his chest. "...you stole *what I could have been*. You stole my life. And why? *Why?*"

Finch stayed in his seat, one hand braced on the arm. The room spun for Finch, but not from the drink.

"You ungrateful... how *dare* you?" Finch said. His voice had become a cold growl. "None of this was yours to steal away. Not the studio. Not the dream. Not even Rosalind. Least of all, her. She was a *mistake* that you weren't willing to admit. And yes, you'd have drowned in the smallness of that life. Huh! You pretending to be a father, and all the while missing all of *this*? Your unused talent, the lost opportunities, watching the world—no, the years go by—would have swallowed you up."

Through older eyes, Finch watched from the sidelines, and he understood. Edmond was not only angry. He was broken. He knew what Finch had done in secret. The conniving. All the slithering around the truth. And he knew, as Finch now did, that some wounds would never close.

Edmond shook with involuntary spasms, and his fists balled into tight knots.

"You've never needed a pitchfork. Just a polished smile and somewhere to hide the evidence," he said.

"Oh, don't lie to yourself. Not now. Don't pretend that you had no idea what happened to Rosalind so long ago. And *you let her go*. You *let me* do what had to be done so you could be... so you could be happy," Finch said. His last words were a whisper. He balled his fist and put it to his mouth. But it was too late.

"Happy...? What in the goddamned hell are you talking about?" Edmond asked.

"You let it happen because you loved me. You *love me*," Finch said. He stood now, his lips quivering like an old man sipping hot soup.

"Oh, no. Oh, my God, no. You're crazy. You're delusional."

Edmond withdrew a revolver from his coat and aimed it at Finch. The gun was small, dull, and dark. Nothing dramatic. "You took my whole future..."

"No, Edmond. *I gave you* a future. You had none without me. Without all this. And yes. You loved me," Finch said. "And goddamn it, *I loved you back*. So now what? Because you're so afraid of the truth, you're going to kill me? Is that it?"

"There's no killing you, Bramwell. You've been dead a long time already," Edmond said. And he pulled the trigger.

The sound wasn't loud. The flash was small, and so was the smoke. Finch felt the bullet strike and rip the breath out of his lungs.

He staggered back and fell into the screening room seats. His face contorted, at first in pain and surprise, then it darkened.

Edmond fled, and he let Finch lie abandoned to his own miserable, undignified end, with his limbs scrambled amid the red velvet. Finch's chest hurt, and there wasn't much room to take a breath. His smoking jacket was wet, and the stain beneath spread. He placed a hand inside the coat flap and extracted a heavy silver flask, the one Edmond bought for him... the bullet lodged in its side.

The Hollywood streets stretched out cold and dark, slicked from a rain that had only just passed. Neon signs flickered above shuttered buildings that ranged down the blocks in either direction. It was midnight. And maybe past that. A low wind howled down the asphalt, catching the hem of Edmond's coat. He staggered to the curb and pressed his fedora down, in case anyone might come by.

There, at the gutter, a sewer drain gaped like a wide cement scream carved into the side of the road. Water poured down its open throat. Edmond ditched the pistol there, and it clattered down, splashing into the sewage below.

Further down the road, much further than Edmond could see, the mechanical bell and clack of a streetcar clattering along the tracks sounded. It wouldn't stop for him unless he flagged it down, and he couldn't afford to do that. Someone would recognize him. Most everyone in this town had seen his pictures in the paper, sunning himself poolside with Vivian Delacroix, Horace Bellamy, and other well-knowns.

His tears blurred the sidewalk. And for a moment, the regret was louder than his fear of consequences. But then it hit him. What he'd done. He looked both ways and then dropped to the asphalt on his stomach, reaching as far as he could into the sewer drain. He realized with a sudden cold dread that the police might look there first.

But it was no use. The storm runoff and garbage it picked up drenched him. The police might ask to see his clothes. Wool wouldn't dry overnight, and he'd not be able to get to a dry cleaner in time. He'd have to ditch everything. Even so, they had tricks now. Nitrate tests. Lab men who could sniff out the smallest trace of guilt. And the gun. Reaching it would be impossible now.

He rolled onto his back and cried aloud for all that he'd done and for all he could not do.

The grind of steel against steel intensified as the streetcar pressed onward. He could feel its vibrations crawling up through the pavement and rattling his bones. His thoughts scrambled as the shriek of the train bearing down from a distance took him from his immediate pain. He staggered upright and waved. He knew the cars were off duty at this hour. This one would head to Grand Central Station, repositioning for tomorrow's routes, just as it did every night.

But he couldn't think straight. He kept his brim low. Maybe the conductor would recognize him. Maybe not. It was so late. But anyone who wasn't drunk would remember a man soaked by gutter water and dripping in garbage who flagged a streetcar down after midnight.

None of it mattered. Not now. A small plan was hatching, born from his desperation and adrenaline.

He'd take the streetcar as far as it might take him. Then he'd hide out.

In the morning, before any headlines, he'd take what he had from the bank and head to Mexico. It might take him nine hours to get to Tijuana in that deathtrap coupe of his. With any luck, he'd be at San Ysidro before sundown.

"Hey!" he called as the streetcar approached. The sound of his own voice startled him. It peeled from his mouth full of madness. He waved both his arms over his head.

The streetcar's headlamp swung up to the sky as it topped the small hill, then it angled down toward him. The bell rang twice.

Behind him came footsteps, crunching against the loose pavement gravel.

Edmond turned. He knew someone had spotted him.

A man was there, half-lit by the trolley's glow. But a scarf covered his face, and an oversized coat engulfed his body. But the eyes. Edmond could see they were wild, delirious, red, and drunk with rage. His coat had a dark stain of liquid soaking through the lining. Blood. One sleeve flapped empty as he limped forward, dragging something in his left hand.

A metal film canister.

"You don't get to decide how this ends," Finch said.

Those were the last words Edmond heard. The canister swung upward in a wide arc, striking Edmond's jaw with the sound of splitting bone. He stumbled backward, and his arms flailed. He caught his heel on the railway tracks and stumbled backward to the ground.

The streetcar's brakes screamed to the stars, but there was no time. And before Finch could edit his work, it was done.

He still clutched the canister while he tore down the street, running as if the night shadows chased him.

The elder Finch stood watching the scene unfold. His excuses had ended. His troubled explanations, his incessant rewrites of every action he'd taken, had darkened with the night sky and folded into a final silence.

The smell of goat pelt and death tarnished the air behind him. He heard the beast gnashing with its teeth, crunching through bones and flesh.

"Moo-oo-re," the goat said.

FIFTEEN

FINCH FOUND HIMSELF IN an apartment. It was tidy, well-organized, and simple. A Christmas tree with few ornaments and just a few strands of tinsel stood by a bay window overlooking the twinkling city lights. Rosalind leaned on the windowsill, sipping from a cup of holiday warmth.

Victor placed an arm around her shoulder, and she leaned on him. Long silver strands wove through her locks. Her eyelids drooped, and her cheeks hung in small scallops. And her face, while still graceful, bore the quiet etchings of time's long visit.

"It's not the same," she said.

"Did you expect it might be?" he asked. "How many years has it been?"

"Six. Six long years." She sighed and straightened herself up. "Well, look at me, still a mess after all that. I think we should open a present or two. That's what the moment needs."

They collected green and red packages from beneath the tree and went to the couch.

"You first," she said. She gave him a smile, but too many troubled ghosts lurked behind it.

Victor smiled back and took his time unwrapping the box. He laughed and extracted a black beret.

"What's this for?"

"I figured since this is your first directing job away from Cine-Film, you should look the part," she said.

"It didn't take long, did it? A little shocking. After all of Finch's work. The whole of CineFilm crumbling like that," he said. "Did I ever tell you how I met him?"

"I'm not sure I want to know," Rosalind said. "If it involves the Rialto, you'll need to get me a stiffer drink."

"I had just finished a picture with Horace and Royal Monarch. And it wasn't exactly a happy sendoff. Horace practically gave me the bum's rush for drinking on set, and rightfully so. Anyway, it was around the same time Finch was setting up for his first picture... Which one was it again?"

"*Dusk Over Savannah.* Oh, good lord. After that picture, Vivian and a handful of other actors swore off Finch forever," she said.

"Yes, well, during that time, I was out of work. But he remembered me. He was so young, but he remembered me from a silent I'd directed in Europe. It was on a park bench he noticed me and right away. He said he'd be a big producer one day, with that carnival-barker grin of his, selling stars that hadn't yet started twinkling," he said.

"I remember that side of him," she said. "Back then, we all thought grit and charm were enough. And maybe they were... for a minute, anyway."

"Well, he saved me. Did you know that?"

"What?" she asked. "How do you mean? He couldn't have possibly...."

"I was hitting the bottle pretty bad. But he promised me a job as long as I dried out. Can you believe it? I was so ashamed that a kid had to tell me to sober up. So, I did. And I never looked back," he said.

"Well, at least one of us can still conjure up a charitable Christmas ghost for old Finch," she said. "All right. Enough. This is Christmas Eve. I won't let that man spoil another moment. Shall I open mine?"

Victor nodded.

She grinned and tore through the wrapping. A silver frame emerged, containing a photo of her and Tim, their smiles bright with a hope she almost remembered, but she had long since pushed away.

She paused, and Finch watched as sorrow filled her eyes. She wiped them.

"I love it," she said. She gave Victor a kiss. "If only he were here..."

"Now, Rosalind. You said yourself it's Christmas Eve... time to be happy, right? I thought this might cheer you up. I'll just have to take it back."

She laughed through the tears. "Don't you dare. I love it. And I love you."

Finch watched, and his eyes stung with what he dared not name. It was the same feeling from childhood he'd had once or twice before his father beat it out of him. But here it was again.

"Surely, I thought Rosalind would have a kinder word for me. After all, we'd..." Finch couldn't finish. That burdened childhood feeling made its way up and choked out the words.

"Shh," Rosalind said. "Did you hear that?"

"Hear what?"

"I'm probably losing my mind," she said.

"Rosalind. Can you hear me?" Finch asked. "Rosalind, please forgive me if you can. For everything."

"Sometimes I think he's still here," she said. She tilted her head and moved in his direction, holding out her arms as if she might touch Finch. "...Like in a character in a movie, only he's just out of frame."

"Still here? What does she mean?" Finch asked.

The goat clutched his shoulder and whipped him around to face a new vision.

It was raining. Four people stood near one another, sharing umbrellas. Finch watched the four of them: Rosalind, Victor, Vivian, and Horace. They had drawn expressions, except for Vivian who glanced at her wristwatch and looked like she had better places to go. Or at least to drink.

They surrounded an open grave. A minister read holy words, but they hung heavier than the rainclouds above.

"Darling, it's a bit too late for that," Vivian said. The minister paused mid-verse. Rosalind nodded for him to continue. Horace gripped Vivian's arm, and she made a face like she'd eaten a sack of garbage.

The minister rushed through his verse as though a director had signaled him to wrap it up.

Rosalind moved forward, her gloves in one hand, the rain leaving tracks down her coat.

"Thank you for coming on such a difficult day. It never rains here. But today, it's fitting. There was a time when I thought he would outlive us all," Rosalind said.

"Yes, out of sheer spite," Vivian said. Horace shot a look of warning at her.

Rosalind paused. "He built something from nothing. But he buried himself inside it."

Victor glanced at Vivian, waiting for her retort, but she said nothing.

"He was brilliant. And impossible. And yes, he loved. At least once he did. I know that now. But he kept it locked away until it festered. Until it turned to poison."

She looked down at the headstone.

"I don't know if he'll ever find peace. But I hope he knows... we showed up," she said.

"Oh, come now," Finch said. He turned to the goat, and though the sight of it shrank his fortitude, he couldn't help take a scoffing tone. "You mean to tell me this damp little turnout is a funeral? Three mourners and a powdered banshee late for a Bloody Mary?"

He paced along the grave's edge, trying to laugh.

"Of course they'd do this to fool me, to mock me. Bravo! Well, your little padded-cell production won't work!" he said.

No one heard him.

The goat remained mute. It watched with its slitted eyes shifting back and forth, always weighing, always measuring.

Finch's smile faded, then his face sank. He looked back at Rosalind, who had bowed her head. Then at Victor, who remained solemn-eyed. The two of them were grayer and more stooped than Finch remembered.

"Darling, can you move things along?" Vivian asked. She slipped the minister a five-dollar bill. "And I do mean that in the most *holy* and mournful way."

Finch paced around the muddy grave. Inside was a casket. Black. No flowers. No one even brought flowers to this crummy little set up.

Then he had a glimmer... a heart-stopping recollection, almost like a dream. But before he could formulate the specifics of this lost memory that was starting to come clear, the goat bleated with one of its half-words.

"Cuu-uut," it said. Its voice trembled and shook.

Those assembled at the graveside stood facing the same direction, with their backs to Finch.

"What is this?" he asked. "Some Greek drama? Have you all gone mad?"

Then, he could not speak. He tried. But his mouth went silent. And his limbs stiffened. An unseen hand held him in place.

The mourners who were assembled moved without sound, no footfall at all. Just like Sister Zagan at Saint Cyprian's. And they pushed the headstones away as though they'd never been anchored to the soil. The graveyard backdrop rolled up with pulleys like a window treatment. Horace picked up the grave pit, folded the painted canvas, and carried it off as though he'd done it a thousand times before.

At the same time, they toted in half-round pine trees nailed into crisscrossed floor stands, they spread flake-soap on the ground so it looked like snow, but they all moved in a deliberate, practiced manner. They'd been doing this forever. Then they wheeled in a weather-worn wood structure, tall as a house, and they disappeared.

The goat spoke again. "Aaak-shuun."

Finch lay in the white powder meant to mimic snow, but it wasn't just for show anymore. The illusion was gone, and winter's frost cut straight to the bone. The sharp smell of pine and the faint scent of fireplace smoke hung in the air.

His hips screamed with sheer agony, his spine and ligaments pulled beyond reason, snapped and broken.

A child's hands gripped his ankles, and he felt movement. His jacket and shirt slid up behind him, exposing his back to the frozen landscape. He stopped. Boots broke the silence with a slow, anguished drag through the snow. The child pulling Finch came close to his face.

"Nathaniel?" Finch asked. Or he tried. But it came out as nothing but a series of whistling wheezes.

Nathaniel gazed down at Finch, unsmiling. The child was just as Finch remembered on the day it all began. His cheeks carried the flush of winter, and his eyes were green and steady, but they also seemed too full of dreadful secrets a child shouldn't know. After Nathaniel was certain Finch had seen him, he continued pulling him by his legs through the frosty landscape.

Finch saw the structure appear above him. Brown boards wrecked by winters past with gappy slats between them. A hay loft with an open door at the top. Then he heard a metallic clank as the room darkened.

Nathaniel went to work packing dried hay around Finch.

While he did, he sang a familiar schoolyard ditty.

"Bramwell, Bramwell, soft and meek,
Walks with a wiggle and pink on his cheek!
Talks like a lady, dressed all neat,
Tiptoe, tiptoe, light on his feet!"

Nathaniel poured a liquid on Finch, and he winced at the stench, remembering kerosine's chemical pungency.

Nathaniel towered above. He struck a match and smiled as he tossed it into the hay. He disappeared from view. The barn door opened and clanked with a final lock behind Finch's head.

Finch wanted to scream. He knew he had to move, to run, but his body would not budge. Those same invisible hands he'd felt before now held him to the floor.

He felt the unbearable sear and heard the crackle of his flesh charring as the rafters above groaned, spilling red and orange into the billowing black. He drew a frantic gulp of air, as though he were underwater for too long. But the ashes and heat scorched his lungs. The heat surged through him, violent and blistering, and from that pain the scream tore loose.

"No! Let me out. Please!" he said. "Let me out!"

No one came. And he still could not move his roasting limbs.

The goat clopped forward, unaffected by the blaze. It stood near, watching Finch burn with its black and depthless eyes. It chewed with ritual calm, as though time had slowed and it alone presided over the offering that burned. In its gaze, there was no judgment, nor pity. Only a detached understanding of the inevitable.

As the orange and black turned red-hot and engulfed him, he screamed louder, pleading for someone—anyone—to come. But the flames answered first, swallowing him in a fury of heat and agony.

"Stri-ii-ike," the goat said. Its strange voice warbled, as if the distant projector were skipping.

The flames stopped, but Finch's body was a seeping mess of charred flesh. Wracked with agony, he could only gasp in shallow gulps, mouthing pleas for mercy.

Vivian, Horace, Rosalind, and Victor returned, their faces turned away. Others followed... familiar shapes, names he might have once known. He recognized them, somehow, but couldn't say who they were to him now. None met his eyes. He wasn't sure what crimes he'd committed against each of them. But something told him he had. And that they remembered.

The only sound he heard was the barn being wheeled off on squeaking casters. The ghostly stagehands tugged on ropes off to the sides, and down unrolled a new backdrop. It was solid black, and along with it, Finch smelled wilted flowers and long-forgotten crowds.

One apparition turned. Her face came into view. Gouged-out, empty pits replaced her eyes. It was his mother, dressed in black mourning clothes. She seemed detached, unmoved, as if following the silent cues of some unseen director.

He opened his mouth to speak, to beg for her help. But only a smoky gasp escaped.

And as he strained for words that would not come, only the thud of his heart and the rasp of his breath filled the empty air. No one else wavered or turned. They moved around him, efficient and unerring, as if their work were to assemble the final design, and he was only one more part to be set in place. The hush pressed close, and he felt, for the first time since childhood, what it was to be small.

A rank odor hit his face. A mix of cheap perfume, old cigars, and sweat. The sound of *boom-tss-ba-boom*, the drums and cymbals sounded through the walls and reverberated through his chest.

Finch found he sat at a cracked mirror in a small back room filled with wigs and skimpy outfits hanging with their feathers frayed and falling loose. He wore a red gown, cut very low, and in the reflection, his face was a grotesque smear of lipstick and rouge.

His heart skipped a few beats, and his breath came fast. He knew where he was. But he could not stop what was happening. He felt those same small hands, invisible. Hundreds of them, forcing his body into motion.

He watched his own hands move toward a nearby handbag. In it he saw a tinted bottle of pills and a syringe. And below that was a musical snow globe with Father Christmas inside. It was the one Lola had handed him in his office with the proud gold emblem: *Marchette of Paris.*

The ghostly hands forced him to twist the snow globe key, and it turned in a doleful circle, plinking out *Silent Night*. He watched his own fingers uncork the pill bottle and press it to his lips. The pills tumbled into his mouth, and he swallowed, gasping for air. He filled his mouth. His hand lifted a glass of dirty water, and he choked it all down.

Then he removed the syringe already filled with a yellow liquid. It was the bottle he'd seen prepared by Nurse Gertrude at his mother's side. The small hands forced him to sink that needle and depress the plunger with his thumb. The room seemed to drift, and the sounds of the drums and bass enveloped him, warped and warm, thick as syrup in his ears.

Before Finch could do anything about it, he was onstage. The spotlights hit him like floodwater.

The band started their boisterous music, and Finch looked for a way to run. When he turned, Lola stood in the wings with a baseball bat, twacking it into her palm.

Finch couldn't run. His feet, his legs would not obey. He observed the audience of hooting men and saw himself among the patrons, sitting with Vivian, witnessing the spectacle.

Lola marched out and wrenched Finch's arm behind his back.

"We got a shy one tonight, gents," she said.

The men laughed.

"You've seen him before. Hell, some of you probably had your backs stabbed by him. But tonight? He gives us *the* big comeback. A little looser, a little lower, but ain't we all?"

The drummer slapped the cymbals to drive Lola's introduction home.

She pulled Finch's arm higher behind his back until he heard his bones snap. The pain radiated across his back and came close to knocking him out.

"Back by delusion, denial, and unpopular demand: he's CineFilm's finest, or what's left of him.... Put your hands together for 'Fifi Forget-Me-Not' Finch!"

Lola released Finch, and his arm hung limp. Then his legs gave out, and he collapsed in the spotlight, undone by the lethal mix he'd taken. He gasped for air, but it wouldn't come. He could feel his lungs tightening, squeezing inward, as though the invisible hands from before pressed the air out of him.

He clawed at the air and reached toward the audience, but the men's laughter rang out, hard and cruel, as if they'd paid well for this show.

The goat stood in the front row, watching with its pitiless gaze.

"Cuuut," it said. The word rattled out like a machine gun.

The uncanny stagehands returned, but the crowd of them had increased in size. More faces of people he'd known and wronged. All of them gliding through the dark and shifting the scene with silent, practiced hands, assembling a new nightmare. A white blindness of death glazed their eyes.

Finch was in a forest again. It stank of damp pine and melting snow. The air tasted cold. He stood in a familiar clearing while his shoes sank into the wet slush. The trees looked too tall now, like they were leaning in, watching, glaring at him for what he'd done and for what dark sacrament they were about to witness.

"Still playing at being a man, Bramwell?" His father's voice floated in the chill like polluting smoke.

Finch turned to face his father. He held a shotgun aimed at Finch.

"Soft as chiffon," his father said. "And twice as delicate."

The same words again. But this time, there was no gun in Finch's hands. All he had to hold was dread.

Panic took him, and he sprinted through the trees. But he heard a click and a fiery round blasting. He felt the shot strike him in the back and burst with a sting of flame through his chest.

He looked down and saw the mess. Bits of maroon organs and bone were everywhere in the snow. Leaking down the front of his coat. His breath was leaving him in broken final puffs. His hands twitched, grasping at the snow as he knelt.

His father approached and gazed upon his handiwork with no discernable expression beyond satisfaction.

"You... you shot me," Finch said.

"Yes," his father replied.

"Get... help..." Finch said. He heard his words bubble through the blood.

"No," his father replied. Then he stepped over his son, his boots slogging through the snow, leaving his only boy to bleed into the white.

The goat watched nearby with its unforgiving eyes. Chomping. Chewing. Blood slipped from between its lips and down its beard. Finch collapsed into the frost. The light drained away.

The spectral crew returned, moving with grim purpose as they reset the scene.

The goat spoke. "Pri-i-int."

Finch stood in the middle of the road. It was night. He'd been here before. Too many times, in nightmare and sleepless terror. He'd made a mistake here. But he had his reasons.

The streetcar's headlamp crested the hill, a trembling beacon in an unforgiving night sky.

The bell clanged once.

He knew what would happen. Footsteps scuffed behind him, measured and slow.

He turned.

Edmond's face looked pale with moonlight, and his eyes shined with a quality Finch could not recognize. Not at first.

"I'm sorry," Edmond said.

"Why?" Finch asked.

Then he saw it. Edmond's eyes shined with pity. Not anger. Not with revenge.

"This is the only way," Edmond said.

"It doesn't have to be," Finch replied.

"But it does," Edmond replied.

He placed a hand on Finch's chest. His touch felt light, at first. Fingers spread. Then his shove was a sledgehammer against Finch's ribcage.

Finch stumbled backward, and his heels struck the streetcar rails.

He tried to catch his balance as the trolley headlight was upon him. The brakes screamed as they had a million times in fevered dreams.

Then the light delivered its pain.

Sixteen

THE MINISTER WAS GONE now. The small group assembled for Finch began trudging through the wet and the cold.

"Thank goodness Samuels was waiting for Finch in the limousine. If it wasn't for him witnessing what Finch had done, poor Edmond's fate would still be a mystery," Rosalind said.

They continued their walk through the rain-sopped grass and tried to avoid sinking soil.

"We really believed Finch, didn't we? That Edmond was spiraling, and that somehow explained what happened to him. But then again, Finch just wrapped what he did inside another story. Lots of people were broken up over the market crash—that was true. But to say Edmond threw himself in front of that streetcar...?" Victor said.

"Don't beat yourself up," Rosalind said. "None of us knew what to think. Finch was better at covering his tracks than we ever realized. He was a producer to the end."

"Poor Samuels," Victor said. "He was terrified to say what he'd seen. Understandable with a man like Finch at his back. You knew how it was. He could ruin anyone for good. Could have gotten Samuels blackballed and then buried without a stone. At least once Finch was gone, Samuels did the right thing."

Finch followed the group. The rain permeated his shoe leather, drenching his socks.

Rosalind's words rang through him and brought him to the brink of tears. But they would not come. It was far too late for that.

The goat followed behind, its hooves thudding in the grass.

"And thank God he did," Vivian said. "Heaven knows who else suffered from that man." She clicked her pearls with her fingernails.

Rosalind spoke again. "And that note. I'm glad the police found it in Finch's desk. I didn't know what happened to it. I was hoping to put things right between Edmond and Tim. But Finch needed to be there, too. He had his part to face. I wanted us all together to lay the complicated truth bare. I thought I'd signed it. But I didn't. And now... it's too late."

Finch turned to the goat, expecting it might say more. "That note was from Rosalind?"

The goat licked its lips and chewed in that slow, endless rhythm, then curled its tongue to draw back a strand of drool laced with blood.

"Oh, my God. I... I lied to myself. And I believed it. Oh, Edmond, I believed it!" he said.

"Did I ever tell you that Tim looked up to Finch?" Rosalind asked. "Said he wanted to be like him one day. I never had the heart to ruin it for him."

She covered her face and wept. Victor stopped with her, holding the umbrella to shelter her, his free arm wrapped around her shoulder.

"The city finally boarded up the Rialto after everything that happened... after everything they found," Horace said.

"They caught those three hoodlums, too," Victor said. "Apparently, Finch had been paying the manager to keep the Rialto clean. No back row hanky-panky, you know? Never asked who did the sweeping. Didn't know the manager paid Frankie and his gang under the table.

"After Edmond was gone, I think the loneliness just... caught up to him. And who wouldn't reach for something? For comfort. For contact. That balcony was Finch's undoing.

"I guess it's easier to pretend in the dark.

"He must've reached for Boyle by mistake. And in the end, Finch got exactly what he paid for."

Victor shook his head.

"I can only imagine Finch's pain... living with all he'd done. Though he never showed it... at least not in the usual ways," Rosalind said. "He always looked that way, come to think of it. Even as a young man. Like he'd done something awful, like a man with secrets waiting for someone to find him out."

The small group dispersed to their automobiles and went their ways.

"The Rialto? What does he mean 'caught up with him'? That's absurd. I've never set a single foot into that place..." Finch said.

But his words faded out, and he glanced away as if remembering some secret he'd kept from himself. The morbid stagehands appeared and rolled in the new scene.

"Rii-all-to," the goat said, its voice trembling like someone throttled it.

The air reeked of bleach, as if it might erase what had transpired. But the stains remained, sunk deep into the grout, like guilt etched where no eye could see. He'd been here before.

Finch's heart fluttered. Then it lost control. He knew where he was, and the stale reminder dragged him back to Edmond. Always Edmond. He couldn't bear to think on him any longer.

He remembered finding his way here that night, after Edmond was gone. He had wandered in, searching for anything that might ease the crush in his soul, if only for a heartbeat. He swallowed hard and tried to summon a trace of saliva.

Everything stuck in his throat, and he felt his grief lodged there forever.

He heard voices just outside the door. He went to the sink and pretended to wash his hands.

Two men spoke.

"I'm afraid this will officially close the joint," the first said. He had a raspy quality, like he chomped cigars for a living.

"But Laraby. There's got to be some arrangement we could come to," the second man replied.

Laraby spoke. "Look, Phillips, you're the manager here, right? Well, take a good look, will ya? Hobos in the park, ten-cent-tarts on every corner, and The Palmetto, where the fellas play a little too cozy for comfort. And now you're operating a nuisance that's had three incidents just this week. Now, if you'll excuse me, I need to make sure the tags are still in order. We expect you'll keep this bathroom locked until we collect the evidence and the coroner comes. You got that?"

The door swung open, and Finch pressed his back to the wall.

Laraby acted as though he was alone. He busied himself with examining the markers on the floor. Finch had noticed none of it until now.

Laraby finished and stepped outside. The door locked with Finch inside.

Finch didn't move. He just listened. The echo of Laraby's footsteps faded, but the silence that followed wasn't filled with peace. It was the kind that waits and knows exactly what it's waiting for.

He noticed the floor where Laraby had worked. There were chalk markings with numbers beside them. One outlined a street knife. A thick redness coated it and ran into the grout.

And there was another. Inside the closed toilet stall, the outline of a leg. There were spats on the shoes. They'd fallen from favor, except with men of a certain age.

His heart swelled with panic. He shook without control. Finch eyed the stall and pressed upon the metal door. It swung inward. There he was, lying beside the bowl, his head twisted to one side without grace. His neck sliced in one clean stroke.

Everything changed in that moment.

The floor seemed to fall away. He hit a surface cold and hard. Metal. Straps bound his arms, his chest, his legs to the table. A sheet lay across his face. He strained against the belts but couldn't move.

The sheet tore away. Sister Zagan stood over him, watching with her slitted, unfeeling eyes. And he understood now. The goat had always been there, in many forms, in many faces. Following. Watching. Waiting.

She smiled, revealing rows of long, jagged fangs. A line of drool with traces of blood in it slipped from her mouth. She withdrew a scalpel from her tray. As she made sharp, clean incisions in Finch's body, she sang like a mother soothing a child. He squirmed in pain.

"Silent night, holy night,
All is dread, no more light..."

Her voice was reedy and off-key. It was Lola's voice. Her words twisted upon themselves in a lullaby of despair.

"Soon you'll be for our feast,
Soon you'll be for our feast..."

The doctor entered. The same doctor Finch had met in the morgue.

"Fine, fine. Excellent work, Sister," he said. "It's like you were born to the task."

He gazed down at Finch and locked eyes with him. He pressed his palm against Finch's eyes and closed the lids.

"Embalming can be tricky. But this is just splendid. Fine indeed!"

Finch strained and forced his eyes to open.

But he was inside the Rialto restroom again.

Nathaniel stood next to the stall with his blackened, crackling skin and his leaking eyes. He moved his mouth and jutted out his charred tongue. He raised a hand and pointed behind Finch.

"Well, isn't this dramatic, Finchy? Gutted in your own theater like some tragic low-budget ingénue," Vivian said.

Finch whipped around, and she stood behind him, martini in hand, sucking along the glass rim.

Finch turned back to face the stall, and the goat was there in front of it, with fresh blood slicking its mouth. The red-brown stain extended longer down its neck than before.

It reached its blood-slicked claw across the stall door. It scratched the metal, leaving crooked gouges and threads of curling paint as the door opened wide.

Orange ash fell like burning snow around him. The stall opened to Nathaniel's barn, engulfed in flames and belching smoke.

SEVENTEEN

TIM AND ROSALIND SAT in the dark of the fictional Screening Room Six, the drapes drawn and the projector clicking and humming on, cold and indifferent to the reel it played of that man's devastation. He'd ruined so many, and now they knew why.

They remained in shadow, sometimes laughing, sometimes crying. Tim had never died. That was the spirits' doing. They wanted Finch to know, to see the legacy of his denial, to etch his soul with the understanding of how he'd touched so many lives with a poisoned hand. Each of Finch's sins played out here, where there was no popcorn, no treat to buffer the devastation.

Rosalind sat closer to Tim and tilted her head onto his shoulder. They would talk more now. There would be no more secrets, now that she could see what he'd not been able to say. Now that he knew his father, and the harm that secrets do.

They found the check made out to Rosalind in his shirt pocket. It hadn't been lost. Fifty thousand dollars would go far, especially now.

They watched the final scene.

The stall door opened wide. Finch had nothing more he could say. He nodded in acceptance. One last inevitable signature on the dotted line before the pact was complete. The goat placed its clawed hand on Finch's shoulder, and together they disappeared into the savage flames beyond.

The projector shook and gave a mechanical note of unhappiness. The film glitched, and a test pattern appeared. After a few beeps, a new image played. It was out of focus at first, but it stabilized.

Finch stood alone while mist swirled around him. It was gray where he was. Everything gray. A shadow moved from deep within the haze. Edmond emerged past the murk. He and Finch stood side by side, just watching them back through the screen. There were no words. Just the ever-present sounds of the projector clicking.

Their faces looked the same as always, but their eyes looked like they'd seen the weight of the world and owned it for themselves.

The two men clasped hands without exchanging glances. Their dismay was palpable. They turned from the camera, and the film bubbled and snapped. The two of them then vanished into the blinding light that remained.

EIGHTEEN

GOLD SEQUINS SURROUNDED THE table near the stage at the Palm &
Pearl Club. The women wore feathered everything, and tables over-
flowed with questionable shellfish. Horace Bellamy leaned toward the
group, still chuckling, but the group at the table remained stone-faced.

"...And then I told him, if the monkey can take direction better
than you, maybe he should be getting top billing."

Vivian rolled her eyes so hard her earrings swayed.

"I didn't realize the time between awards required both a calendar
and a sedative," Vivian said. She tipped her glass toward her lips then
stopped with a gasp. "Darling, a martini without an olive is like me
without an award. May I borrow one?" she asked.

Tim nodded, trying not to laugh. Rosalind elbowed him to keep
him from Vivian's wrath.

Vivian reached over, and instead of pulling the toothpick-skewered
olive from his glass, she downed his entire drink in one gulp and placed
the remaining olive in her own full cup.

Nicky wanted to say something but instead raised a finger for a
refill. He and Tim looked like polished ebony in their shining tuxedos.

Horace blinked at her and raised an eyebrow.

"What've you got to complain about? You've already won," he said.

Vivian glanced down then took a dramatic little inbreath as she
stroked the cold metal statuette.

"Oh, *that's* right. And isn't it beautiful?"

She lifted it to eye level, fogged it with her breath, and polished it on her breast.

"And to think, I don't remember filming a single scene."

Horace sipped his highball. "You never do. You know, you could probably go home now if you wanted."

"What? And miss seeing Carrington Black lose *Best Picture* for the third year in a row? I may never get this lucky again," she said.

A man came from the wings carrying an envelope. He had hair as black and slick as a new car's fender.

"Ladies and gentlemen. This has been an exceptionally unusual year of cinema, with several fine contenders for Best Picture and, as you know, a few last-minute darlings making their way to the ballot box. The judges have concluded their tally, and hearty thanks go to the entire Motion Picture Guild for their tireless efforts.

"This year's nominees include *A Kiss Before Midnight* from Horace V. Bellamy and Regal Monarch Studios, the stirring tale of an heiress who finds her heart tangled up with the very man who tries to take her life; *Dead Letter Office* from Carrington Black and Metropolis Pictures, a gripping drama of a Minnesota mill worker whose life is turned upside down by a mysterious stranger; and *Dark the Halls* from Rosalind and Timothy Crisp and CineFilm. A potentially biographical film, depicting a ruthless film mogul who views haunted reels of his past sins and is forced to confront the ghosts of a career built on betrayal, regret, and ruin."

The audience offered a patter of mannered applause.

"And the winner is... *Dark the Halls*, Rosalind and Timothy Crisp for CineFilm."

Tim and Rosalind swept up to the stage and gripped their awards.

"Thank you," Rosalind said. "This film..."

She stopped, her voice catching under the weight of it. She glanced at Tim, then out to the crowd, and wiped at her eyes.

"This film began as a very personal project. It took a lot for us to obtain this story and to bring it to you in all its haunting truth."

She held the statuette a little closer.

"Some men don't just die once," she said. "Some die slowly. Over decades. One shame at a time. And if our little production helped you see something important, then remember it. You may need it before the lights go down."

The audience stood with a lengthy ovation.

Tim leaned into the microphone.

"And might I add: a Merry Christmas, everyone."

About Timothy Roderick

Timothy Roderick is a native of Southern California and lives in Los Angeles. He is the author of five acclaimed nonfiction works, including the COVR finalist Wicca: A Year and A Day (Llewellyn, 2005); Wicca: Another Year and A Day (Llewellyn, 2015); Apprentice to Power (Crossing Press, 2000); and the Small Press Award winner Dark Moon Mysteries (Llewellyn, 1996), which was also a Time-Warner Book of the Month Club selection. His first book, The Once Unknown Familiar (Llewellyn, 1994), established him as an influential voice in contemporary Pagan literature. His work has also appeared in The Witches' Calendar, Llewellyn's Magical Almanac, The Encyclopedia of Wicca and Witchcraft (Llewellyn, 2000), and A Witch Like Me (New Page Books, 2001).

In recent years, Roderick has turned to fiction, drawing on folklore and psychological suspense. His folk-horror novel Cornbones (2024) was ranked among Malevolent Dark's "Best Horror of 2024." He is also the author of Nine Zero One Three (2023), One Crooked Thing (2020), and the young-adult fantasy Briar Blackwood's Grimmest of Fairytales (Lodestone, 2015).

If **Dark the Halls** lingered with you, I would be grateful if you shared that experience with others. A simple star rating or a few words on Amazon, Goodreads, or your bookseller's site can help guide future readers to this story's door. Independent publishing depends on voices like yours to keep its light burning.

With gratitude,
Timothy

Also by Timothy Roderick

Cornbones

Henry Rustin thought he was escaping the mob. Instead, he found something far worse in Harveston's fields.

★★★★★

December 2024: Best of Horror, *Malevolent Dark Magazine*

Nine Zero One Three

Haunted by childhood trauma, Rachel knows the past can't be buried—it must be fed.

"Claustrophobic dread... Mr. Roderick knows his way around the English language and he uses it evocatively..."

★★★★★

--Facing North

One Crooked Thing

It whispers from mirrors. It watches his child. And it won't stop until it takes his soul.

"Suspenseful and intense!"

-Amazon review

★★★★★

Briar Blackwood's Grimmest of Fairytales

Behind the door waits curses, monsters, and a queen bent on Briar's destruction.

"A heroine's journey in a gloriously imaginative world."

-Amazon review

★★★★★